BEST FRIENDS, WORST LUCK

Mary Hooper knows more than most people what makes a good story – she's had over six hundred published in teenage and women's magazines, from *J17* to *Woman's Own*, and she tutors evening classes in Creative Writing. In addition, she's the highly regarded author of over fifty titles for young people, including *The Boyfriend Trap*, *Mad About the Boy*, *The Peculiar Power of Tabitha Brown* and the Spook stories (*Spook Spotting*, *Spooks Ahoy!* and *Spook Summer*) about Amy, a girl with an overactive imagination. Mary has two grown-up children, Rowan and Gemma, and lives in an old cottage in Hampshire.

BEST FRIENDS, WORST LUCK

MARY HOOPER

WALKER BOOKS

AND SUBSIDIARIES

LONDON • BOSTON • SYDNEY

First published 1992 by Walker Books Ltd
87 Vauxhall Walk, London SE11 5HJ

This edition published 2001

2 4 6 8 10 9 7 5 3 1

Text © 1992 Mary Hooper
Cover illustration © 2001 Sue Heap

The right of Mary Hooper to be identified as author
of this work has been asserted by her in accordance with
the Copyright, Designs and Patents Act 1988.

This book has been typeset in Sabon

Printed in Great Britain by
Cox & Wyman Ltd, Reading, Berkshire

British Library Cataloguing in Publication Data:
a catalogue record for this book
is available from the British Library

ISBN 0-7445-8290-3

CHAPTER 1

"Don't use that phone!" Mum said, as I crept down the uncarpeted hall. "We stopped paying for it at nine o'clock."

I *had* been making for the phone − robbed of its table and sitting on the floor.

"All the better, then," I said. "I can ring Sal for free."

Mum tutted, made a groaning noise, then, obviously deciding that she couldn't be bothered, passed by me, carrying a huge heap of stuff − sheets, books, pictures, a brass ship's bell and some coat-hangers. Two forks fell from her as she passed.

I picked up the phone and dialled Sal's number, feeling miserable. This would be the very last time I'd be ringing my best friend from here. At eleven o'clock − or whenever every last coat-hanger had been loaded into

1

the removal van – we (Mum, Adele and I) were moving. Going to live on a *farm*, of all places. No *wonder* I was fed up.

Sal answered the phone in a muggy voice, which meant that I'd got her out of bed.

"This is the very last time I'll be ringing you from this house," I said pathetically.

"It's only half past nine," she complained. "I was asleep."

"I've been up since six," I said. "Not that I was *sleeping*. I was on the floor of the living room in a sleeping-bag and the zip kept sticking into me."

Sal yawned. "Got everything done then, have you? Packed up?"

"Nearly," I said, trying to ignore the thought of fifteen little piles of things which I couldn't find homes for sitting on the floor of Adele's and my bedroom. Or what used to be our bedroom.

I hesitated; I knew I was going to wish I hadn't asked, but I couldn't resist it. "What are you going to do today?"

"Dunno. First day of the holidays. . . I'll just lollop around, I suppose. Might go swimming this afternoon with Donna and Roselle."

A quiver of jealousy ran through me. I picked up one of the forks and jabbed it into the furry felt underlay stuff stuck on the stairs. She was going off with them already!

"It's not warm enough," I said.

2

"It might be, later."

"Thought you didn't like Roselle..."

"I've got to have someone to go round with, haven't I?" Sal said in a reasonable voice.

"Well, couldn't you..." I trailed off. I didn't have any suggestions as to what she could do without me around to be her best friend. Except curl up and hibernate, perhaps. Or at least stay in for a decent period – say, a year, preferably dressing only in black.

Mum came past, carrying a pile of boxes. "Have you got all your smelly soaps packed?" she asked. "The last time I saw them the cat was lying on them in the broom cupboard. And you haven't let him out, have you?"

I grimaced down the phone. I had, actually, let the cat out, forgetting Mum's instructions not to. Well, there had been so *many* instructions.

"Are you still there?" Sal asked, as Mum passed by.

"Only just," I said gloomily. I removed the fork from the matting. "When are you going to write to me, then?"

"Next week – or whenever I've got something to tell you."

"I'll write as soon as I get there," I said. "That's if they've got letter boxes. They probably communicate by carrier pigeon."

Sal gave a snuffle of a giggle. "Go on. It

can't be that bad. You've been before, haven't you?"

"Afraid so," I said. Adele and I had been down there twice. And I don't just mean down from London to Somerset (where the farm was). *Down* on the farm. You say that, don't you? Like *down* in the dumps and feeling *down*. There had to be a link there somewhere.

"It'll be nice," Sal said. "Cows and things. Lambs," she added vaguely. "If you bottle feed them, they follow you around."

"He hasn't got lambs," I said.

"He's all right though, isn't he?"

"S'pose so," I said. *He* was Mum's new husband; we'd met him loads of times. His name was Roger – Adele and I called him Podger because he was fat.

"Well, then. It'll be good. Exciting!" Sal lied.

"You wouldn't say that if it was you who was going," I said. I wriggled the fork right under the felt matting. "You will come down and stay with me, won't you?"

"Course!"

"When?"

"You're not even there yet!"

Suddenly, from upstairs, came a dreadful scream from Adele. "Beverley! If you've taken my spotted socks. . ."

"You'd better go," Sal said.

4

"Oh, it's only her going on about her stupid clothes again," I said, carefully unrolling the offending items from my feet. "How about coming down to stay next month?"

"Could do," Sal said. "Though there's Donna's swimming party in August – and Mandy's having a disco."

I jabbed the fork so that the prongs came right up through the top of the felt matting and tore it. At that moment two things happened: Mum came by with a clipboard, said, "For God's sake!" and pulled the fork out of my hand; and Adele appeared at the top of the stairs and bellowed, "If you're wearing my socks and my new pink pants I'm going to kill you!"

"I'd better go," I said, hastily rolling the sock-ball to a dark corner of the hall.

"See you, then!" Sal said, and was gone before I could extract any agreements as to *when* I'd be seeing her and for how long – or make her promise to stay my best friend for ever, no matter what.

Adele thumped down the stairs, wearing an old dressing-gown of Mum's. Adele's sixteen and has straight gingerish hair, a very pale skin and freckles. I don't look anything like her – thank God. If there's one thing I can't stand (apart from farms) it's freckles.

On Adele's face was her full *Kill Beverley*

expression, which I hadn't seen for a good two weeks, come to think of it. Weirdly enough, and for the first time in our lives, we'd been united – in our general hatred of farms and going to live on them. Now, though, hostilities had clearly restarted.

"I left the clothes I was going to wear today in a neat pile in the bathroom," Adele said threateningly. "One new pair of pants, one bra, one pair of jeans, one T-shirt, one pair of socks."

"So?" I said.

"Now the socks and the pants are missing. And all my others are packed so I've got none to wear."

"So why should I have them?" I said, wriggling on the stairs – Adele's knicker elastic was digging into me.

"Because you always take everything of mine!"

"Gross exaggeration! I do not! I don't even *like* most of your clothes."

Mum came back, ticking things off on the clipboard. "For goodness sake, aren't you dressed yet?" she said to Adele. "The removal van has just arrived. The men are coming in to start loading."

Adele gave a scream and tried to spring at me.

"I haven't touched your socks and pants!" I said, crossing my fingers. "But if you like,"

6

I added in a goody-goody voice, "I'll help you look for them."

"The cat!" Mum said, all anguished. "Someone *must* have let him out."

I stood up. "Right, I'll get things sorted." I pretended to search around the hall for a bit, then pounced on the socks. "There we are!" I said. "I thought I saw the cat playing with something."

Adele snatched them up without so much as a thank you. "I suppose," she said, heavily sarcastic, "the cat rolled them up into a little ball himself, did he? And now I suppose he's gone out wearing my pants!"

"Actually, I did see him wearing a pair of..." I began, but the two removal men came in just then, rubbing their hands and saying they wouldn't mind a cuppa – and Adele fled back upstairs.

It was all a fuss about nothing. Adele had loads of underwear; she was always buying it with her Saturday job money. And it wasn't even as if they were particularly comfortable pants – and if I couldn't find any because Mum had packed everything of mine, what was I supposed to do?

While Adele was in the bathroom I wandered into our bedroom. Our beds had already been taken to pieces and were stacked against the wall; our clothes were in suitcases and black plastic sacks; and there were piles of homeless objects scattered around, waiting to be claimed. Most of them were mine. There were some old school text books which should have been returned and a pile of letters on paper torn out of our rough notebooks: letters from Roselle or Sal or Donna along the lines of, "*I don't like you any more. I'm not going to be your friend and I'm going to go round with . . .*" etc. As well as these, there were a few smelly soaps that hadn't got into the broom cupboard pile, some of my favourite books, a heap of yellowing photographs cut out of *Fast Forward* and *Smash Hits*, a few bits of make-up purloined from Adele, and some cassettes and LPs.

There was an already-bulging (but still open) black plastic bag in the corner of the room. I pushed everything of mine into this and then, hearing Adele coming out of the bathroom, decided it might be a good time to go and look for the cat.

I disappeared out of the back door while mum was fussing at the front and started calling, "Puss . . . puss . . ." – loud enough for the cat but not so loud that Mum would hear and start carrying on about me having let him out. I went out of the gate, trying to remember the last name he'd had.

Mum had bought him ages ago, when she and Dad had got divorced; I think he was a sort of substitute for a man about the house. She'd

8

called him Felix, Adele had called him George and I'd called him Lucky (he was black). Then Adele had gone off George and started calling him Luke, and I'd gone off Lucky and started calling him Possom – until the cat hardly knew which way up he was. In the end we'd all just called him "the cat". It was easier.

"Puss . . . puss . . ." I called again, looking into hedges and up trees. There was no sign of him, though. The cat, quite obviously, had got wind that we were moving and had decided to leave home. I didn't blame him a bit. Who in their right minds would want to move to a place consisting of cows and mud? Not only that, but a place a million miles away from all their friends? Given half the chance, I would have run away, too.

There weren't many people around, and as I cat-hunted I thought pathetically that this was the last time I'd be walking on *this* pavement, see *this* tree, trip over *this* broken kerb. I tried to conjure up a deep sense of betrayal, but it was difficult because we hadn't been living there that long. I mean, I couldn't pretend it was my childhood I was losing, or anything dramatic, because we'd only come to live in the place four years ago, when Mum and Dad had got divorced, sold the other house and split the money.

I hadn't minded moving then, because Mum had lured me with talk of my new school having a swimming pool, an open-air theatre and a fast-food style canteen: it had sounded so much more exciting than my old school that moving hadn't mattered To make things even better, I'd made friends with Sally on my first day there and we'd been best friends ever since. Most of the time.

I walked through the recreation ground, came out the other side and looked cautiously down the road towards Roselle's house. Suppose I saw Sally going round there right now, unable to wait another minute before she got a new best friend?

Everything was quiet, though. There wasn't as much as a cat – any cat – in sight. I walked back through the recreation ground, kicked the roundabout, jumped on a crisp packet and smiled politely at a neighbour who gushed, "Bet you're excited about moving!" at me as if I were eight years old. Going back to the house, I surprised the cat who was washing his bottom right outside our front gate. I swooped on him.

Carrying him into the house, I found the cardboard pet carrier Mum had bought, and stuffed him into it. Much to my surprise, he went in quite nicely: there was just one quick yowl of protest as I fastened the top down.

"I've got the cat, Mum!" I said, as she passed me with two black dustbin sacks full of who-knew-what.

"Good, good," she said vaguely. "Now, go and help Adele with the last of the upstairs stuff. There are two strong cardboard boxes up there and I want you to empty everything from the bathroom cabinet into them."

I left the cat trying to put a paw out of the cardboard air-hole at the front of the box and went upstairs to our ex-bedroom.

"Did you find your pants?" I asked Adele, managing to sound as if there were a distinct possibility that she might have.

She rounded on me. "No, I didn't! And now I've got to go two hundred miles in the car with no knickers on!"

I was just going to say that it didn't really matter because she was wearing jeans, when one of the removal men put his head round the door. "Hope it won't be draughty, love!" he said cheerily, and Adele gave a short scream, went scarlet, rushed back into the bathroom and locked the door.

I paced about in our bedroom a bit, thinking that some sisters had absolutely no sense of humour, and then I positioned myself outside the bathroom.

"Mum says could you fill those two boxes in there with everything out of the cabinet," I said through the keyhole.

"Has he gone downstairs?"

"Who?"

"The removal man, stupid!"

11

"Course he has."

The door opened so abruptly that I almost fell in. Adele strode out, stony-faced, went into our room and started tying up bundles of books. "I've never been so humiliated in my life," she said. "And if I find out that you're wearing *anything* of mine..."

I crossed to the window quickly, all the better to change the subject. "Just think, Dell," I said – I used to call her Dell when we were little – "it'll be the last time we'll look out of this window, and the very last time we look out at houses." I shot a glance at her; she still had steam coming out of her ears. "The next time we look out of our bedroom window it'll be at ... at *scenery*."

"And mud," she said.

"And cows..."

"And more mud."

"There'll be trees and – " I searched my mind for other things you found in the country – "grass and stuff."

She came and stood by the window. "I'm going to hate it," she said in a wobbly voice. "I know that James Baker won't write to me – I've only been out with him twice. I'm going to miss his sister's Eighteenth and he'll more than likely dance all night with Alison Peters. I won't have *anything* in common with anyone down there; I'm not even going to speak to them. They'll all be wearing flares."

12

I nodded miserably. "Sally will go off with Roselle and Donna and they'll decide they don't like me," I said. "I've got to go on a bus to my new school and wear a brown and mustard-coloured uniform. I'm going to hate everyone."

"I *hate* cows," she said.

"So do I!"

"And mud," she said despondently.

Mum's voice came shrilling up the stairs. "Have you got that bathroom stuff packed yet? I want to leave in ten minutes!"

Adele and I stared at each other in anguish. Ten minutes! Ten minutes of civilization left, and then we would be wading in cow-pats and chicken droppings for the rest of our lives...

CHAPTER 2

"Not much further," Mum said over her shoulder as we turned into a lane with tall hedges on each side.

I sat up and tried to look interested. We'd been driving for about three hours and I was in the back seat, half buried under lost property and cat carrier. I shook the carrier a bit in order to warn the cat that we were approaching his new home. He'd been really good all the way down – which was a great improvement from when I'd taken him on a trial run to the supermarket: he'd been sick on the way there *and* the way back. I felt a wave of fellow-feeling for him. Poor old puss! He'd been forced into the country too; uprooted, torn away from all his friends...

"Nice field mice coming soon!" I said temptingly. "New furry things to chase..." He didn't seem impressed; didn't give as much as an answering miaow. I stared out of the window; I wasn't impressed, either. Just as Adele and I had said, all there was was *green* things. Fields and trees and hedges and banks and grass. Not a sign of a shop or a café or a cinema or a school or a community centre holding an under-16s disco every Friday. What would I *do* all the time? Anyway, even if there *was* something to do, who would I do it with now that I was all alone in the world and completely friendless? There was no one to moan to, no one to go shopping with, no one to talk to about music or clothes, or what pigs older sisters were. I was – I struggled to think of a tragic enough word – like an *orphan*. Only with no friends instead of no parents.

I stared at my reflection in the back window, making my eyes look large and mournful, trying to produce a few tears. If Mum looked in her driving mirror now, she'd probably be so stricken with pity that she'd send me back to London immediately to live with Sally's mum and dad.

"What have you seen out there?" she suddenly asked. "It's obviously something interesting – your eyes are as big as saucers."

"Nothing!" I said hastily. "Nothing interesting. Green things, that's all."

She and Adele resumed their talk on Personal Relationships – it was very boring –

while I worked on a new and even more tragic look. Suddenly Mum said, "Here we are! Here's the village!"

"Where?" I asked, my head moving from side to side like a Dalek's.

"We just passed it!"

I turned and stared out of the back window. All I could see was a couple of rows of little houses, some bigger ones standing on their own and a petrol station.

"Is that *all*?" Adele asked.

"The village green is just round the corner," Mum said. "There are quite a lot of houses there, and two pubs and an old church. And there's a new estate, too."

"Oh," said Adele, and she half turned in her seat and gave me a *My God What a Dump* look.

Mum turned into the driveway of the farm. There were two Land-Rovers and a tractor standing in the yard, plus several wooden cart things and some bits of machinery.

From the outside the house looked like a typical farmhouse, I suppose. It was a big, old, flat-faced building, with eight or so windows at the front. Next to it, attached at each side, were sheds and outbuildings and things that might have been stables. A bit down the lane was the proper farm, where the cows lived in the winter and went to be milked, and where their feed was stored in huge barns.

"Here we are!" Mum said, just as Adele heaved a big sigh. I clutched the cat carrier to me. My only friend! I would take a new interest in the cat, in . . . in Possom. I would talk to him and tell him my troubles.

"Leave everything where it is for now," Mum said. "We'll sort things out in a moment."

The door of the house opened and Podger came out, smiling all over his fat face.

"Good afternoon, girls," he said, as I swung my legs out of the car and stepped straight into my first bit of chicken dropping. (I assumed it was chicken.)

Adele and I nudged each other while I furtively wiped my trainer on a bit of grass. *Good afternoon*, indeed! Why did he have to be so formal?

Mum flashed us a look. "Hello," we muttered obediently.

"Welcome to Much Standwick Farm," he said, giving a little bow, and I might have giggled with embarrassment if I hadn't been so fed up.

Mum and Podger kissed each other – just on the cheek, nothing too snoggy in front of us. He was taller than her and had a beard which was going grey, hair that was going grey and a big stomach. He certainly wasn't anything to write home about, but Mum seemed to like him.

"Did it all fit in the van?" he asked, putting

an arm round her shoulders. "Everything go all right?"

Mum nodded. "Not too bad at all. The girls were a great help."

Adele and I looked at each other; we knew she was only saying that so we'd get off to a good start with Podger. She'd already told us he might be a bit awkward because he'd not had any children of his own. "He won't know what to expect," she'd said. "You'll all have to make allowances for each other."

"When will the van get here?" Podger asked now.

"They said about four o'clock."

"So you've got a couple of hours to relax. Come in and have something to eat."

We left everything in the car – I even left my one friend in the world – and went inside. There was a shoe-scrapy thing at the door and without even looking at me Mum said, "If you've got anything on your shoes, Beverley, please scrape it off."

I scraped and went in. The kitchen was quite modern, but it had one of those cooking ranges with big circular discs that you lift to put the saucepans under, and an oven thing you have to put logs in. The units around the walls were pine and there was a big pine table, but there were no curtains or carpets and the whole place looked cold and bare. Mum had said that the house lacked a woman's touch.

Podger had been married before but he'd got divorced years ago, so the woman's touch must have worn off. Or maybe she'd taken it with her.

Adele and I stood around in the kitchen feeling awkward, while Mum started busily looking into cupboards and muttering to herself.

"I expect you girls would like to see your rooms," Podger said, rubbing his hands. "They're a bit basic at the moment – I've left it to your mum to go and buy what curtains and stuff you need, later."

I was just going to say that I wanted to see mine, when I heard a sniff from Adele, and when I looked over she was *crying*.

Mum heard the sniff at the same time. "Darling!" she said, rushing over to put her arms round her. I rolled my eyes to myself.

"Want to come and see your room, Beverley?" Podger asked hastily, so I nodded and followed him into the hall. The stairs were all closed in and very steep, with no carpet, and they led on to a gallery which had all the bedroom doors coming off it.

"Your mum and I thought you'd like this room," he said, and he pushed open the door next to the bathroom. I'd seen it before, of course, when Mum had shown us round on one of our other visits, but I couldn't really remember it. It was quite small and the ceiling

19

went up in a point, and opposite the door it had one large pointed window to match.

It had a bit of scrubby carpet on the floor and there were some shelves in an alcove, but apart from that it was completely empty.

"Very nice," I said politely. I searched my mind for other polite expressions. Comfortable? Cosy? Actually, it looked about as comfortable and cosy as a larder.

"It'll look different when you get your things in, of course," Podger said, "and at least you won't have to share with Adele."

I brightened up – just slightly. It might be worth living in a larder just to get *her* off my back. We were friends now, but I knew it wouldn't last. In fact, I could see it finishing pretty swiftly a bit later, when we got undressed...

He showed me the other rooms – Adele's was bigger than mine – and we went down again. Adele was still sniffing and Mum was patting her.

"Bit strange for them," Mum explained to Podger in a low voice. "There was lots going on at home that they've had to leave: friends, their social life, you know. Adele had a new boyfriend and..."

"Mum!" Adele protested.

"Lots of boys down here!" Podger said jovially. "There's a new estate just down the road."

20

Fresh tears came into Adele's eyes. "As if . . . as if . . ." she said in both a scornful and a tearful sort of way.

I knew what she meant. She'd said it often enough: as if she could ever fancy any farm boys, *country* boys, wearing checked shirts, flares and wellies.

I looked at her, thinking that she was probably having nearly as bad a time as me – but that at least she wouldn't have to go to a school where you wore a brown and sick-coloured uniform. I moved my chair nearer hers in a slight show of sympathy, and Mum looked at me fondly. "At least it's made my two girls appreciate having each other," she said to Podger. "I've always wanted them to be closer, and now they are."

I wriggled on my chair uncomfortably. *Yuk.* Mum was speaking as if we were about to start walking round with our arms round each other and calling each other "Sis".

Podger rubbed his hands together again. "Tea, everyone?"

"I hate tea," Adele and I said together.

Mum sighed. "Adele only drinks instant coffee with evaporated milk in it and Bev only drinks orange," she said. "There's both in the van but of course . . ."

"Evaporated milk . . ." Adele said suddenly. "Where's the cat?"

"Still in the car," I said.

Mum gave a small shriek. "Poor thing!"

"He's all right," I said. "I've been looking after him. He slept all the way down."

"Go and get him in now, then, Bev," Mum said, "while I sort out something to eat."

I went outside, looking round carefully for chickens and wild animals as I crossed the yard. There was enough muck around for a whole *zoo*.

I hoicked the cat carrier out from the pile of lost property. Adele's silk skirt, which she'd demanded be laid on top of everything and not squashed in a case, came out with it, snagged itself on a rough piece of the door and fell on the ground. I picked it up hastily, shook it out and shoved it back. If there was the slightest thing wrong with it, I'd be done for.

I stood in the yard for a moment, wondering what Sally was doing. If she'd gone swimming with Roselle and Donna they'd be at the baths now. They'd more than likely have met up with some of the others from school; they'd have taken sandwiches and be sitting having a picnic and a laugh. I bet Sally wasn't missing me a bit...

A faint miaow came from the cat. While I'd been thinking about Sally, I'd been twisting the cat carrier round from side to side, so the cat probably thought he was on the Whip at the fair.

"Bring him in!" Mum called from the door.

"Don't let him out in the yard – he'll run away."

I slammed the car door shut and was just crossing the yard when there was a strange whirring and hissing and scuttling noise and a herd of *huge* grey duck things ran round the corner, all flapping their wings and jerking their necks forward as they swooped towards me. God, it was awful; just like a horror film.

I was going to get pecked to death!

I dragged the car door open and leapt back in, shaking all over. When the things got to where I'd been standing, they stopped dead and began hissing and making evil noises at the car as if they'd like to peck through the door.

I crouched down low on the seat, thinking that I wasn't going to move an inch until they'd gone, even if I had to stay in the car all night. After a moment or two Podger came out and shooed them round the corner and away.

"Sorry about them," he said, opening the car door. "They wouldn't have hurt you, though. They're just my guard geese."

I picked up the cat again, made a dash for the farmhouse and sat down shakily at the kitchen table. "I thought a goose was a nice fluffy white bird with a yellow beak," I said.

"That's Goosey-Goosey Gander in the

nursery rhyme," Mum said. She smiled. "Still, you cheered Adele up. She said she hadn't seen you move so fast since she told you she'd lost a chocolate Easter egg down the back of the settee."

"I'm glad someone enjoyed seeing me almost get eaten alive," I said bitterly.

I put the cat carrier down on the floor. "We have to put butter on his paws," I said. "I saw it on *Blue Peter*. We butter his paws and then he sits and licks it off and by the time he's finished he feels at home."

"Is that right?" Podger said. "What if he just runs off with buttery paws?"

I frowned. "They don't," I said. As if my best friend in all the world would do that, anyway . . .

Mum bent down and opened the door of the carrier. "Out you come, then, Felix!" she called encouragingly. "Out and see your new home." He didn't move. I gave the box an encouraging tip to one side. "Possom!" I called.

"Luke!" called Adele.

He appeared very hesitantly, blinking in the light. "Here he is!" I said, rather pleased with myself. I'd found him, I'd looked after him all the way down and now he was going to be my best friend.

Adele gasped. Mum gave a little shriek. "Beverley!" they both said, looking at me accusingly.

"What?" I said, niggled. Some people were never satisfied. "He's all right, isn't he? His fur's a bit bedraggled but..."

"*It's the wrong cat!*" Mum said.

"That's not *our* one!" squealed Adele.

The cat looked up at us.

"Course it is," I blustered. "Yellow eyes ... black fur. Course it's ours."

"It's Mrs Armitage's cat!" Mum said. "It's our Felix's cousin."

"Don't be daft..." I said uncertainly. But now that I looked at this one properly, I could see he wasn't *quite* the same.

"Poor Mrs Armitage," Mum said. "She'll be going quite demented. You know how she dotes on her cat."

"Well, she can have ours!" I said. "I don't suppose she'll even notice." I looked at them. "It'll be all right. We'll take over *this* one and she can have ours."

"Ours won't go to Mrs Armitage's," Mum said. "Ours will just sit outside our old house..."

"And starve!" put in Adele.

"I'll have to ring someone," Mum said. "Really, Beverley. I would have thought you'd have known your own cat."

"Well, I..." And then I had a brilliant idea. "I know. I can take this one back and bring our one down!"

"I don't know about that," Mum said.

25

"I'll do it!" Adele interrupted. "I'll go next Saturday."

"No, I should go!" I insisted. "I made the mistake so it should be me who has to go."

I brightened. I just might get delayed up there and have to stay with Sally for some time. . .

CHAPTER 3

Dear Sally,

How are you? Not all that different from yesterday, I don't suppose. Well, I've survived my first night in the wilds. No bears broke in in the night and carried me off.

It was really hectic yesterday, what with unpacking and sorting out my room (I've got my own bedroom!) so no one went to bed before one in the morning. I was looking forward to a good lie-in, but there was no chance of sleeping beyond six – that's the time everything starts mooing and hooting and twittering and cock-a-doodle-dooing.

Here, something mad has happened – Adele has packed the wrong cat! Instead of our one we've got Mrs Armitage's. Mum tried to ring Mrs Armitage last night but she's ex-directory or something, so she had to ring someone else to go round and feed ours. In the meantime, do you think you could go round and see Mrs Armitage and just ask her to ring my mum? Say that we'll return her cat (Mum says it's called Fluffy Bo-Jo!) as soon as we can.

About returning it. I'm working on Mum to let me bring F B-J up and collect our one. I thought I might come one Friday AS SOON AS POSSIBLE. Like on day of Donna's party. What do you think? I tried to ring last night to ask, but everyone was out. Write back quickly and let me know.

It's awful here. Boring. The village consists of about one house and half a shop. I've got to go out with Mum later and I'll post this if it's one of the days that the letter box has a collection. Adele hates it as well. We have to talk to each other because there's no one else.

Did you go swimming yesterday? How were Donna and Roselle? Did they say anything about me? Who do you like best out of them?

Well, I'd better go; I've got various things of Adele's around the place and I want to hide them before she barges in and starts playing private investigators.

Write immediately on receiving this letter.

28

Love from your faithful best friend,
Bev x x x

I addressed the envelope, found some clothes of Adele's and stuffed them into one of the washing bags, then got dressed and went downstairs. Mum was pottering in the kitchen, humming to herself.

"All right, darling?" she asked. "Sleep well?"

"Awful," I said grumpily, then remembered what Adele and I had said to each other last night – that we would try, as much as we could, not to let Mum know just *how* much we hated it.

"We want her to be happy, don't we?" Adele had said earnestly. "We were pleased when she met Podger."

Remembering this, I turned a sigh into a cough. "Not bad," I said to Mum. "I could hear animals and things early this morning, though."

"Oh, you'll soon get used to country noises," she said cheerfully. I stared at her; she was wearing an *apron*; I'd never seen her in one before. Her hair was down and she looked as if she might produce a home-made cake at any moment.

"Where's Roger?" I asked.

"Oh, he starts at five o'clock," Mum said. "Farmers do, you know. Now, you and I are going to the shops this morning. Roger's got some strange ideas about housekeeping and I want to stock up the cupboards." She turned and gave me a beaming farmer's wife sort of smile. "Nice new-laid egg for breakfast?"

"Yes, but if you think I'm going outside with a little basket looking under hedges, you've got another think coming," I said heatedly.

She looked at me in amazement. "Why ever should I want you to do that?" She opened the fridge and took out a Sainsbury's box. "We haven't even *got* any chickens here."

"Good!"

"Although I might ask Roger if we can have a few. It doesn't seem like a real farm without chickens clucking around, does it?"

"It seems quite real enough to me," I said gloomily.

"No sign of Adele moving around upstairs yet?"

I shook my head.

"You know, we're all going to have to make a special effort with Adele."

"Why's that, then?" I moved from chair to chair around the table like baby bear, trying to decide which place to adopt as my own.

"Because she's really upset at having to leave that boy. That James someone."

"Mmm..." I said, yawning and settling myself at the top of the table, with my back to the window so I wouldn't have to look outside.

"So be especially thoughtful towards her, will you, Bev?"

"Oh, sure," I muttered. So let me see . . . that was me being thoughtful to Podger, me being thoughtful to Mum and me being thoughtful to Adele. Who was going to be thoughtful to *me*, that's what I wanted to know.

Mum slipped a fried egg on a plate and turned from the cooker thing. "Oh – that's Roger's place – if you don't mind, darling . . ."

I took Sally's letter with me to post when we went down to the village. Mum carried two shopping baskets and pointed out places of "interest" along the way.

"The man who lives there's a schoolteacher, and the lady who runs the post office comes from that house," she said out of the side of her mouth as we went along. "*That* place used to be a blacksmith's forge – just imagine!"

I looked and I couldn't imagine because it was now a ladies' hairdresser's: *Giovanni, Late of Rome.* Stuck on the window were photographs in various stages of yellowness and peelingness, showing hairstyles which were "The latest from Paris" (ha ha) or (under a bouffant affair that I recognized

from Mum's wedding photo – *first* wedding)
"à la mode".

I sniggered loudly and Mum nudged me.
"Quiet! Someone might hear you."

"I'm not going *there* to have my hair
cut!"

"Don't be silly, you don't have to. I'll take
you and Adele into Taunton."

"Or..." I looked up at Mum hopefully,
"I could have it done at home – I mean, in
London – when I take the cat back."

"We'll see," Mum said.

We passed some front gardens – Mum
remarked on the flowers: how beautiful they
were; lovely rich Somerset earth; could never
get flowers to grow like it in London, etc. We
passed some rickety old houses which looked
as if they'd fall down if you slammed the front
door – Mum remarked how quaint they were:
full of old beams; same people been living in
them for generations, etc.

I sighed. I just couldn't see what she
was going on about. Everything was *old*;
everything was *quiet*; everything was *boring*.

"About the cat," I said.

"What about him?"

"*Our* cat. I expect he's really missing us.
He might be off his food. I bet Mrs Armitage
isn't feeding him properly."

"Of course she is. And since when have
you been bothered about the cat? You can't

remember what his name is, much less recognize him."

"Well, *anyway*," I said firmly. "I really do want to go back and see everyone." I looked up at her plaintively. "I haven't got any friends here . . . no one at all."

"Give it time, Bev," she said. "We've only just arrived and I think it would unsettle you to go back straight away. Besides, you'll make friends here really quickly, I know you will. I bet as soon as you start your new school there'll be someone nice for you to be friends with."

"How could anyone wearing a brown and sick-coloured uniform be *nice*?"

We walked the long way round, circled the village green. (Mum said that that was where they danced round the maypole on May Day and where next month's big village fete was being held.) Past the pubs, we approached a mini-roundabout. One of the roads off the roundabout led to the estate of new houses, Orchard Green.

Mum pointed down towards the estate. "There. There's bound to be some young people living *there*," she said. And we were about to cross the top of the estate road when, as if to prove her point, one of the nearest front doors opened and two girls about my age came out. They began to walk up the road towards us.

33

"There you are!" said Mum with satisfaction.

I studied the girls out of the corner of my eye as we crossed over their road. One was plumpish and dark, with thick curly hair, dressed in jeans and – yawn yawn – one of those hooded tops that went out years ago. The other was smaller, dark too, but with long straight hair and a straggly fringe that looked as if it might have been got at by Giovanni, late of Rome.

"Now, they're about your age," Mum said. To my horror, she'd slowed down a little and was smiling in the girls' direction.

"Mum!" I said, looking with pretend interest at a brick wall. "Come on!"

"Don't you think it would be a nice gesture if we stopped and had a word...?"

I gritted my teeth. "No, I don't! I'll die if you stop..."

"I could ask them if they'll be going to Bigg's Hill Comprehensive – and where the bus goes from."

"You'll do no such thing!" I said, going scarlet at the thought.

She was still dawdling. "Or we could at least introduce ourselves and say..."

"Mum! I ... I'll kill you if you speak to them. Come *on*!"

The two girls had noticed us now – well, I suppose new people in the village were roughly the same as visitors from Mars anywhere else. As I urged Mum on, away from the round-about, they turned into our road and fell into step a way behind us. I could feel their eyes *boring* into my back. I knew they were taking apart my jeans (luckily I was wearing Adele's 501s), my trainers (the absolute latest from our market in London) and a white T-shirt with the latest sort of slogan (no slogan) on it. They couldn't fault a thing I was wearing – not that *they'd* know anything about fashion anyway.

I increased speed, dragged at Mum's hand to pull her along, but she was in a silly mood and swung my hand up in the air. I heard a giggle behind us and dropped it hastily. *Now* they'd think I was the sort of girl who walked to the village with her mum *holding hands*.

"What gorgeous hollyhocks!" Mum exclaimed, looking in a front garden and falling back again.

"*Come on!*" Next time I came out with her I'd put her on a lead.

We reached the so-called High Street with the two girls hot on our heels. They were whispering, and I just knew they were whispering about me. Luckily the "general store", as Mum called it (actually, a poky shop), was just on the corner, and I got in there as quickly as I could.

"How lovely! Sweets in old-fashioned jars!"

Mum said as she came through the door, and my heart sank. We'd be here hours while Mum went through the entire stock, cooing and marvelling about everything.

We saw the girls again on the way home. They were sitting on a wall, chatting to another – older – girl, wearing a dress with *fringes* on (how embarrassing!). As Mum and I passed, a complete silence descended. As we walked on down the road, lugging a ton of shopping, this time I knew that *three* pairs of eyes were boring into my back.

"There!" Mum said when we'd passed. "They seemed all right, didn't they? I don't know why you didn't say hello."

"Because I didn't want to," I muttered.

"I thought you wanted to make some new friends?"

"Not *them*!" I said fiercely. "Not anyone down here."

Adele had managed to get herself out of bed by the time we got home, and was sitting in the kitchen drinking coffee and talking to Podger.

"Roger said we can go and watch the cows being milked when we like," she said to me.

Oh, big deal, I thought. "Oh, really?" I said. I edged towards the door; I'd just remembered I was wearing her 501s and wanted to get them off quickly.

"You'll come, won't you, Bev?"

36

"If you like," I said, disappearing up the stairs, faint with astonishment at her asking me to go somewhere with her. Usually she couldn't get rid of me quickly enough.

I put on my own jeans, rolled up Adele's and put them in a corner of her room, and went downstairs again. Mum and Podger had gone into the yard and were chatting about something.

"What's the village like?" Adele asked.

I rolled my eyes. "Dead!"

"Anyone interesting? Anyone my age?"

"No one you'd like," I said. "A girl wearing a dress with fringes on."

Adele gave a scornful laugh. "Say no more."

"I was thinking," I said. "Maybe we could both go up and take the cat back."

"Why?" she asked suspiciously.

"Well, I don't think Mum will let me travel up there on my own, but she wouldn't mind if we both went together. We needn't stay together once we're there – I could stay with Sally and you could stay with Marcia or someone."

Adele – the new, improved, friends-with-me Adele – nodded slowly. "Mmm. Maybe we could." She sighed. "I can't go on much longer without seeing James . . ."

I nodded and assumed a sort of under-standing expression – just as if I did, although I honestly couldn't see why anyone would be fussed about not seeing *him* with his funny hairstyle and leather jacket he never took off.

Mum came in, opened the door of the washing machine and started hauling things out.

"I've found lots of things we thought were lost," she said, dropping the wet stuff into a washing basket. "Two T-shirts of yours, Adele. And those knickers you made such a fuss about..."

She held them up. "They were in one of the black sacks."

I put on a smug, self-righteous expression. "See!" I said. "I *told* you I didn't have them."

"Well, OK, you little rat, how did they get on their own from the bathroom to a black plastic sack?" Adele narrowed her eyes and instantly reverted to not being friends with me. "And how strange that those two T-shirts are ones that you've borrowed in the past..."

"I don't know what you're talking about," I said with dignity. "I really feel that an apology is in order."

Adele gave a snort and I hopped out of the room quickly. I went upstairs and stared out of my bedroom window, which overlooked the lane that went past the farm. I looked out at the fields and pretty flowers and trees and stuff, and wished with all my heart that I was back looking over rooftops and television aerials and distant factory chimneys.

Maybe I'd try and ring Sally again. . .

CHAPTER 4

"Has the postman been?" I asked Mum, step-
ping over Mrs Armitage's cat, who was curled
in front of the oven thing. We hadn't seen him
for three days after we'd first arrived; he'd
set up camp under one of the chairs in the
sitting room and only bothered to come out
to "excuse himself", as Mum put it. Now he
looked quite at home – which was no reason,
of course, not to take him back as soon as
possible.

"I'm sure I saw the postman," Mum said.
"He didn't call here, but I saw a red van go
by the end of the drive."

I considered this news. "Well, do you think
he knows we live here yet?" I asked. "Maybe
some letters have arrived, but because he
doesn't know our names he's not delivering
them."

"Of course he knows we live here," Mum said. She pushed a poker into the oven and raddled around the logs a bit. "In a small village like this everyone knows when new people have arrived – *and* what their names are."

I sighed and sat down to the breakfast that Mum had laid ready for me. Sally had had *masses* of time to write. I calculated carefully on my fingers: I'd posted my letter on Tuesday, so say it had reached her on Thursday and she'd written back as soon as poss, like I'd asked, it would have got to me by Saturday. But now it was Monday and I still hadn't heard from her. We'd been living in Much Standwick a week. A whole week without communication from the outside world. Seven days away from civilization as I knew it.

"Why don't you *ring* Sally?" Mum said suddenly.

"I have," I said gloomily.

"And what did she say?"

"Nothing. She was out." I pushed a bit of dry muesli around my plate. "Both times."

"Didn't you leave your number and a message for her to ring you?"

I shook my head.

"Why not?"

"Because," I swallowed, "because when I spoke to her mum the second time she said she thought Sally was out with Donna –

41

and because if I give her my number and she doesn't ring, then it'll be much worse."

"Oh, Bev..." Mum said, in the sort of voice she'd once used when I'd fallen off my three-wheeler trike. "I do wish you wouldn't rely so much on her. Start to think about your new life down here a bit. Maybe you could join the Brownies or something..."

"Brownies!" I said, my voice rising to an anguished squeak.

"Well, the Guides, then. Or the library. Or anything that'll get you out so that you start to meet girls your own age."

I pushed the muesli away. "I don't want to join things!" I said.

"Now you're being childish," Mum said with a sigh, and I remembered I was supposed to be being thoughtful to her. But I really couldn't be bothered to be *anything*. I left my breakfast and – looking carefully around for the geese first – went into the yard to be miserable in peace.

It was all right for Mum; she was positively blooming down here. She'd got flowers in vases all over the house; she'd put frilly check curtains on poles across the kitchen windows; she'd planted herbs in an old wheelbarrow, and whenever she went out she took a book of wild flowers with her and kept pouncing on little bits of weeds and things and pretending they were rare specimens.

42

I picked my way carefully across the geese poo in the yard and went to sit on the sunny wall. I decided that I'd stay there until the afternoon post (if they had one) – or the geese – put in an appearance. If I stayed in view the whole time then the postman, as he went by in his little red van, might suddenly remember that he had a letter for me.

I stared down the lane, past the farmyard where the cows trooped in and out to be milked twice a day, towards the village. It was so *quiet*. How could anyone live here without going round the bend?

I suppose I'd been sitting there about half an hour, just brooding, when Podger drove into the yard in his pick-up truck.

"I've got something for you!" he shouted, jumping down out of the cab.

Unless it was a ticket back to London I wasn't really interested, but Mum came out of the kitchen, all smiles, and I knew I'd get blasted if I didn't go over and look enthusiastic about whatever it was. We hadn't seen a lot of Podger, actually. On two separate days we'd been shopping in Taunton for duvet covers and curtains and things, and another day we had put the curtains up, and then there had been our books and records to unpack and stuff like that. Staring out of the window and waiting for the postman not to come took quite a lot of time, too.

Podger let down the end of the truck, picked something – a white animal – out of it and plonked it straight on me.

I was so startled – no, frightened, to tell you the truth – that I dropped it, upon which it landed on four feet and baaed at me.

"A lamb!" I said, and Podger and Mum burst out laughing.

"That's my girl!" Mum said, and Podger said that I was a real townie and no mistake.

I looked again. It was a *goat* – or rather a baby goat, a kid. There was another one, too, the twin of that one, and a big and rather fierce looking fully-grown one with horns. The one I'd been given ran back to the big one. "Well, I couldn't tell at first," I said indignantly. I stared at the animals. "What are they for?"

Podger started laughing again.

"They're not *for* anything," Mum said. "I just said to Roger that it would be nice to have a goat round the place. You get lovely yoghurt from a goat," she added.

"We always used to have an old nanny," Podger said, "but she died a couple of years back. When I saw this one, with her two kids, at market, I thought it'd be nice to have a family. They're no trouble, goats aren't."

Adele came running out in her dressing-gown and I gave myself a hasty check over, but wasn't wearing anything of hers.

44

She put on a silly, soft expression. "Baby goats! Aren't they sweeeet!" she said.

"There's one each for you and Bev," Mum said, "and I'll have the nanny. They're going to live in the barn."

"Aaahh!" Adele said, crouching down and trying to pat the nearest kid, which immediately ran behind its mum.

"Which one are you having?" Mum asked me.

I shrugged. "Don't mind. They're both the same, aren't they?" I didn't really care. They looked quite sweet, but having a goat struck me as about as interesting as having a cat – not very interesting at all.

"I want this little sweetie!" Adele said, and although it went against my better nature to let her get anything without arguing about it, I let her have her way. We took the goats into the barn and Podger told us that the nanny would have to be tied up if the barn door wasn't shut – and so would the kids – but that we could take them to the field at the back every morning and let them out.

"They'll eat scraps – anything," he said – just as Adele let out a shriek. The nanny had its head in her dressing-gown pocket and was halfway through eating a letter.

"Oh no! My letter to James!" she said, and fled indoors. Mum and Podger went in and I was left staring at the goat family. Or goat one-parent family.

"Here, nice goaties..." I said nervously, and took a few steps towards the one that was probably mine (they both looked the same). But the mother put its head down and made a threatening noise, breathing a horrible earth-and-poo smell at me. I stepped out of the way hastily, retreated to the other side of the barn door and looked at them over the hinged top.

You get lovely yoghurt from a goat, Mum had said. *How?* I wondered. A vision came to me of Mrs Goat on her hind legs saying, "*Now which would you like, my dear — strawberry, apricot or fruits of the forest?*" But even I didn't think it was that simple. You'd have to *milk* it first, then do something to the milk so that it would change magically into yoghurt. And if the yoghurt tasted anything like that goat's breath smelt, then you could keep it...

CHAPTER 5

A couple of days later, Adele and I went to see
the milking parlour, which was what Podger
called where the cows went to be milked. We
quite enjoyed the walk down: we complained
all the way about how hateful it was living
in the country, and vied with each other
to see who could come up with the worst
things. Adele promised that, over dinner that
night, she'd tie Mum down to a definite date
for returning the cat. Next weekend, I was
aiming for. I *must* have heard from Sally by
then.

When we got there, the cows had already
come in from the field and were waiting in
a fenced-off bit of the yard. I'd seen cows
in fields before now, of course, but I'd never
actually been so close to a whole lot of
them. They were bigger than I'd thought,

and smellier. They stood placidly, all facing towards the place where they were going to be milked, just mooing and pooing occasionally.

I shuddered. "*Eugheer!*" I said to Adele. "How revolting."

"Look at their *bottoms!*" Adele said.

Podger came up and we tried to look less revolted and a bit interested. Mum had told me that he hoped one of us would take an interest in the farm and maybe go to agricultural college later on. Ha ha.

"They go eight at a time into the parlour," Podger told us. "And there they get their hindquarters washed down and are attached to the milking machines. They're given a highly concentrated feed cake to keep them occupied while they give milk, and their yield is monitored. Do you know, our top cows give eighteen litres a day!"

"Fancy," Adele murmured, while I just made polite noises of surprise, not knowing if this was good or bad. Well, if he'd told us instead that they gave (a) a teacupful or (b) eight hundred litres a day I'd have been just as impressed. Whatever he said, it was all the same to me; I still couldn't see how these big smelly creatures could be connected with the waxed packets of milk Mum bought in Sainsbury's. Or used to buy before she went "country".

"Now we'll go round the back, past the lagoon and through the back door, and you'll be able to see them being milked," Podger said. We dutifully picked our way across the yard.

"Lagoon!" I said to Adele. Visions of blue pools surrounded by palm trees came into my head. "D'you think it'll be like a real lagoon?"

It wasn't. Its real name was a slurry lagoon.

"What's slurry?" I asked, but when we reached it and smelt it, I knew without being told.

"The muck-spreader comes and fills up his little tanker here and then spreads it all over the growing crops," Podger said. "It's a lovely rich fertilizer for the fields."

"Yuk," Adele and I said softly together.

We looked at the refrigerated milk tank, at the cows' overnight and winter houses, at the stocks of cows' winter food which was called silage and the barn with bales of hay, at the water tower, feed concentrates and fertilizers. Let no one say that we didn't look as interested as we possibly could.

"There you are then, girls," Podger said, when he finally let us out. "Fascinating stuff, eh?"

"Fascinating," Adele lied, and I muttered something vague.

49

"Any questions?" he asked, just as if we were at school.

I thought deeply. "All we've seen are cows," I said. "Where are the . . . er . . . man ones?"

"Stupid!" Adele said, and Podger laughed. Someone else laughed, as well. We were standing beside the fence which faced on to the lane and I clearly heard a giggle coming from the other side.

"*Bulls!*" Adele said.

"I know!" I said indignantly. "I forgot the word, that's all!"

"That's a good question, actually," Podger said. "We used to have a bull of our own . . ."

"Just one?" Adele asked.

"Just the one. He caused so much trouble, though – he had a real fierce temper – that we sold him at market and now we just take the cows to the vet when we want to get them in calf." He grinned at me. "So we've just got lady ones here now."

I nodded, hot with embarrassment, thinking about who it was who'd laughed on the other side of the fence. I bet I knew. As we'd walked into the farmyard I'd seen two figures on the other side of the road crouching down behind the hedge. I'd seen them skulking about the day before, too. It was those two girls . . .

We went out through the animal stalls which Podger had called the nursery, just in case any calves had been born in the last half hour (they hadn't). Then Adele decided she wanted to go to the village to get some sweets. I'd had quite enough fresh air for one day, so thought I'd go home – and as I turned I saw the two girls dodge behind one of the farmhand's cars parked in the lane.

It *was* them again; I *bet* they were spying on me. Trying to look as nonchalant as possible, I carried on my way towards home, knowing I'd have to pass them.

As I approached, they came out from behind the car, grinning all over their faces. They sat on the front bumper with their legs straight out, so that either I had to step over them or go right round. I got nearer and they stared at me, staring me out. I stared back. I practised various speeches in my head: "*What are you staring at?*" and "*Nothing better to do than follow me around?*" but in the end I just said in a superior voice, "Are you supposed to be lying all over that car?"

Quick as a flash, the straight-haired one said, "It's my brother's!" and the curly-haired one said, "So there!" and they both giggled. I gave them each a withering look, and gave the straight-haired one an extra-withering look because – oh horror – she was wearing a purple, *nylon* T-shirt.

I carried on walking, conscious of not really having won that round, and behind me heard one of the girls – I think it was the curly-haired one – say, "Have you seen any man cows around lately, Gina?" and the other reply, "No, not at all, Marie. There's a distinct lack of man cows about here today." And they both screeched with laughter.

I gritted my teeth and walked faster. I hated it here; *hated* it. I'd never fit in. Mum would *have* to let me go back and stay with Sally. Adele and I would go to London next weekend . . .

Adele was down at the village for hours and hours – I couldn't think what she was doing – but as soon as she came into the yard I ran down to see where she'd been and what sweets she'd got. She'd been so long, though, that she'd eaten them all. Or so she said.

"What are you going to say to Mum?" I asked. "Let's plan the campaign."

"What campaign?" she asked.

"The going back to London campaign," I said impatiently.

"Oh, *that*." She stared bemusedly towards the shed where the goats were. "You know, I wonder if we ought to be so hasty, Bev."

"Whaat?!" I screeched.

"Going back to London so soon, before we've given this place a chance . . ."

"B-but . . ."

"If we go running back, we're never going to make friends here, are we?"

52

I stared at her, horror-struck. "You don't mean that. You promised you'd ask Mum!"

"But that was before..." She hesitated. "You see, I was down at the village shop just now and I started chatting to this really nice girl, Madeleine, who's working in there for the summer."

"Are you sure she wasn't the one wearing the dress with fringes on?" I demanded.

"Don't be ridiculous. Anyway, when the shop closed she asked me to walk back with her and meet her family, so I did and there's three sisters and a brother," – a big smile slipped over her face – "and the brother's called Mark and he's absolutely gorgeous."

"But you said ... you said all boys down here would be wearing wellies and have bits of straw in their mouths and home-knitted tank tops!"

"*He* hasn't," Adele breathed. "And he's fantastic looking, too. And well ... now that I've seen *him*, the fact that I've had to leave James doesn't seem quite so terrible."

"But you said, you promised..."

"So maybe we won't dash back to London after all."

"Well, you ... you..." I stared at her hatefully, unable to think of anything bad enough to call her. How could she? How *could* she just change her mind like that – how could she *not* want to go back to

London after all we'd said about farms and everything?

"Don't take it too bad, Bev," she said.

"I will!" I shouted, and slammed indoors.

As if *that* weren't bad enough, the next morning I got the letter I'd been waiting for. Except it wasn't what I'd been waiting for...

Dear Bev,

Thanks for your letter. Sorry I haven't written back earlier but I've been really busy. Mum keeps dragging me off shopping for the new school uniform and I've been swimming a lot. We've all joined the swimming club at Martin's outdoor pool.

I've been to visit your cat! Mrs Armitage really likes him. She says she's in no hurry to have hers back, because hers was "temperamental" and yours isn't. She says that Felix (that's what your mum said he was called) has settled down a treat.

We went to a disco at Donna's cousin's house which was great. Her brother came with three of his mates and they were really funny and ever such good dancers. Everyone wants Donna to invite them to all the parties now. I am having a video party (not for anything in particular) next weekend and they are coming to that. There's a new video shop open in the high street and the tapes are really cheap.

We all went roller skating last Friday. Talk about a laugh! I started off quite well, but then Roselle made me laugh so much that I couldn't stand up, and after that I was useless. I know you've never really liked each other much, but Roselle can be quite fun sometimes.

It must be weird being friends with Adele. I can't imagine my sister actually speaking to me. Is Adele really missing James? I expect she'll be coming back to see him, won't she?

It doesn't sound too bad down there; I expect the animals are nice. In the vet films they are always delivering lambs and things; have you helped with any births yet? My mum says all that fresh air must be lovely and to tell your mum that they're trying to stop lorries coming down the high street. That's interesting, isn't it?

Oh well, I'd better go as the others are calling for me and I'm not dressed yet.

Write soon, love from Sal x x x

I read the letter twice, and then I looked on the back of the pages and at the envelope in case I'd missed a PS. There was nothing about me going up there! Not a word. Not a mention of her missing me and looking forward to seeing

me in London as soon as I could possibly make
it . . .

I felt like scrunching the letter up but I
knew I'd want to read it again, even if it
was to wallow in misery and remind myself
how busy not missing me she was, so I folded
it and put it under a pile of books. Then I
went downstairs.

"Nice letter?" Mum asked. "How is
everyone?"

"Oh, *fine*," I said witheringly.

She turned to look at me. She was standing
on a chair and hanging bunches of what
looked like grass – but was probably some
very special rare herb – from the ceiling.
"What's happening up the smoke, then?"

"Oh, nothing much. Everyone's joined
the swimming club, everyone's going roller
skating, everyone's inviting this really fun
group of boys everywhere, everyone's getting
videos from the new video shop and inviting
everyone else to their video party. Oh, and
Roselle is being *such* a good laugh."

Mum smiled. "You wouldn't be exagger-
ating a little, would you?"

"No," I said.

She climbed down from the chair. "Anything about her coming down or you going
up there?"

"No!" I said again.

"Oh well," she said. "Maybe it's just as

well. I'm sure it won't take long for you to settle down here. There's the village fete soon – that'll be a good opportunity for everyone to get together."

Brilliant, I thought sourly. A village fete. And how was I supposed to get together with people when they didn't want to get together with me?

CHAPTER 6

Late one morning, I wandered into the kitchen for breakfast, only to find Mum was busily clearing everything away.

"I want the table to myself for a couple of hours," she said, "because I'm going to do Roger's accounts. If you want something to eat perhaps you'd like to take it somewhere else – somewhere out of the way."

"I'll eat it in the barn if you like," I said huffily.

"I shouldn't, dear. The goats would take it," she said, spreading files and papers all over the place.

I made myself a couple of pieces of toast accompanied by lots of sighing and crashing of the butter dish, then took them outside to eat, intending to get rid of the crusts on the goats. As I walked towards the barn, though,

I heard voices coming from inside.

"And how long did he go out with her, then? What was she like?" That was Adele. I slowed down, ears flapping.

"Oh, he wasn't ever really keen on her," came another girl's voice – I knew who. "Quite honestly, she threw herself at him. It was at a party last Christmas and he couldn't get out of it."

"Really? I can't stand that sort of girl, can you? What did she look like, though? What colour hair?"

"Oh, a really awful blonde colour. Out of a packet, of course. He *loves* red hair, though, I know that. He's always fancied girls with red hair."

"Oh," came Adele's voice. "Is there someone else around here with hair my colour, then, or do you just mean that he . . . ?" She stopped suddenly, because as I'd approached the barn the goats had started to bleat and jump about. "Someone's out there!" she said, and she looked over the top of the half-door and saw me.

"What are *you* doing, creeping about?" she said, narrowing her eyes.

"I just came to see the goats."

"And to earhole a bit!"

"I'm not the slightest bit interested in anything you're talking about," I lied. "I've got better things to do."

"Oh yes? Looks like it," Adele said.

The bottom of the barn door swung open to reveal her new friend, Madeleine, sitting there. Again! Since they'd met in the sweet shop a week ago, she'd practically moved in.

"God! Younger sisters are a pain!" Adele was permanently and fully back to being an old bat again. "How is anyone supposed to have a proper adult conversation with *them* creeping about trying to listen to what you're saying?"

"Marie's worse!" Madeleine said. "When I was going out with Martin Hogarth last year she used to hang out of the window when we were saying goodnight. I've never *been* so embarrassed."

I made a face at Adele and nibbled along my toast crust as the barn door got slammed in my face, top and bottom. After a few seconds, though, the top half opened again. "Take the goats into the field, will you," Adele commanded.

"Take them yourself!"

"It's *your* turn. It was your turn yesterday as well and I did it! If you're not going to do your bit I'm going to . . ."

"All right, keep your hair on," I said, and went in, untied the goats and started leading them out. As soon as I'd got outside, the barn doors slammed again and I heard muffled giggles.

I walked across the yard, scuffing up dust. So Adele had found herself a new best friend – *and* a new boyfriend, by the sound of it – and now she was perfectly happy living in the back of beyond; she didn't want to go back to London to return the cat (who didn't want to be returned anyway) so everyone, except me, was perfectly happy. Well, wasn't that *nice*.

I scuffed along crossly and the dust flew up in clouds and coated my feet. It had been so hot the last couple of days that I'd consented to come out of my trainers and was "letting the air get to my feet" as Mum put it. The goats ran along beside me, pulling in three different directions – the big one, luckily, was behind me, down wind, so I couldn't smell its breath. The kids – Adele's one was called Griff and mine was called Gruff, though we couldn't actually tell them apart – hadn't reached the smelly breath stage yet; perhaps it would come later.

I let myself out of the gate and walked down the track that led to the small back field. I had to pass the geese on the way, but they took one look at the goats and didn't make any attempt to run at me, just stretched and flapped their wings and hissed.

I put the goats in the field and sat on the gate and watched them for a bit. They were quite nice, I supposed – the little ones skipped

about and jumped and played and all that –
but they had a very limited show and it soon
got boring. Once you'd seen them jump on
the big one, leap round and sniff each other's
bottoms a few times, that was it: you couldn't
sit watching them all day.

I jumped down, walked right across the field
and into another. They were all Roger's fields,
I knew. I'd learned enough about farming to
know that the cows sort of circulated around
them, eating them up as they went. I spotted
a couple of houses further down, in a bit of
a valley, and I walked towards these, picking
off bits of hedge as I went along.

Mum would be pleased – I seemed to
be exploring. She was forever urging me to
"go and explore". It was something to do, I
supposed. Another day gone – twenty-two
to go, and then I'd have to get dressed in
that yukky uniform and go off to the new
term at a school where I wouldn't know a
single soul. And at the same time Sally and
Donna and fun-girl Roselle would all start at
Abbey together.

I couldn't understand it. *Why* hadn't Sal
asked me to come up and stay with her? Or
why hadn't she mentioned coming down to
stay with me? Because she was having too
good a time without me, that was why –
and because she liked having the undivided
attention of Roselle and Donna, as they both

fought to see who she was going to be friends with the most.

I walked through another gate and shut it behind me with a crash. There were cows in this field and they stopped chewing, lifted their heads and stared at me. I pushed myself against the hedge a little. I didn't mind cows, I wasn't *frightened* of them, but I hadn't actually come face to face with many – and I didn't know what they might do as a herd. Did they get over excited? Did they ever gang up? Suppose they thought they were bulls and wanted to toss me up into the air?

I tiptoed silently along, keeping close to the hedge. It was a long, narrow field and the cows were scattered all over it. As I walked, some of them spotted me and began to lumber over, still chewing. Other cows, seeing them move, began to lumber over too. When I looked round I saw what seemed like a thousand cows all coming towards me in an attempt to cut me off from the gate at the bottom of the field.

I increased my pace – so did they. I broke into a run – so did they. I began to run faster, stepped in something indescribable and, not bothering to look and see what it was, at last reached the gate and leapt to safety.

The cows stopped dead, disappointed. Some of them mooed. I clung to the gate, breathing fast. That had been a close thing; they'd definitely been going to do something to me.

I examined my foot. *Yuk!* I'd trodden in a cow-pat; a particularly evil-smelling and squidgy one. It was all over my sandal and squelching up between my toes. It felt revolting – and a fly had just landed on it.

I jumped down on the far side to the cows and tried to wipe my foot and sandal on the grass. I couldn't do much, so I walked on, thinking that I might find a stream. I was now in a lane which led to the two houses I'd been heading for – and presumably back towards the village.

I suddenly froze. I could hear voices – giggly voices – coming from round the bend in the road. Oh, I knew who it was. And this time *I'd* spy on *them*...

I looked all round and then pushed myself through a gap in the hedge back into a field. There was just enough room for me to get underneath the wire which ran round the top.

Still as a mouse, I waited, and after a moment the two girls appeared. Both had identical Donald Duck T-shirts, which made me feel miserable all over again – last summer Sal and I had always worn matching T-shirts when we'd gone out together. They were both carrying long stalks of corn, and they were waving them about and tickling each other with them.

I'd wait until they passed, I decided, then

trail them, keeping on the far side of the hedge.

They passed, talking about someone called Miss Summers – "Miss Summers is a right old bag" – and I turned, still crouching, and began to creep along just behind them.

Well, I might have been OK but my foot slipped into a rabbit hole or something and, to stop myself falling over, I grabbed for the wire fence.

"Oww!" I screeched as a great shock ran down my arm. I'd been electrocuted! It was like the shock I'd had once from Adele's hairdryer – but worse.

"What's that?" one of the girls said, and though I thought about doing another sort of "Oww!" and trying to make it sound like a bird call, they'd put their heads over the hedge and were staring at me.

"It's *her*!" the curly-haired one said.

"The new girl!" said the other one. I tried to look casual and nonchalant, as if it was an everyday occurrence to be discovered, electrocuted, sitting in a hedge. "So?" I said.

"What were you doing?"

"You were spying on us, weren't you?"

"No, I wasn't," I said. I stood up, brushed myself down and climbed through to the road. "I was just out for a walk and I saw you coming and I thought I'd hide."

"Nice walk," the curly-haired one said,

pointing at my foot, still caked with cow-pat. "And wire fences, in case you don't know, are usually electric – to keep the cows from straying. You should know better than to go round grabbing hold of them."

"Well I don't," I said. "And I don't intend to learn. I'm not aiming to become one of you lot."

"You speak funny," said the straight-haired one.

I looked at her witheringly. "Actually," I said, "it's *you* who speaks funny."

"Where d'you come from?" she asked.

"London," the curly-haired one answered for me. "Madeleine told me."

"Is Madeleine your sister?" I asked, startled, and she nodded.

"She's at the farm with my sister," I said.

"Yeah. I think she's moved in."

"Are you Marie, then?" I asked, and she nodded again. "I heard them talking about you."

"Oh, Madeleine's always talking about me. Old bat."

The other girl turned her back and tugged at Marie's arm.

"Come on! We haven't got time to stand around talking to *her*." She waved her stalks. "We've got to find some proper corn yet."

"What d'you want those for?" I asked.

"Gina's going to make corn dollies. For the

66

fete," Marie said. Only the corn's not ripe enough and we can't find the right sort."

"Oh." I didn't have the least idea what corn dollies were. They sounded something typically twee and countrified.

"See you," Marie said as they wandered off.

"Cheerio," I said, and they both giggled.

"Oh, cheerio!" I heard Gina saying in what was supposed to be my accent.

I stared after them. Stupid twits! At least I knew their names now, though. And stupid names they were, too.

I climbed back into a field and, avoiding cow-pats and electric fences, wandered home. I'd write to Sal, I decided. And I'd ask her point-blank if I could come and visit.

Dear Sal,

Mrs Armitage's cat isn't settling down at all well and as we all miss our own one, I was thinking of coming up on August 15th with Fluffy Bango or whatever its name is. It would be OK if I stayed with you, wouldn't it?

Things are just the same here and I'm getting to know the animals a bit. They are OK apart from the cows and geese. Adele and I have got baby goats of our own now; they are quite nice but don't do much.

67

Talking of Adele – talk about two-faced! – all of a sudden she's fallen madly in love with some boy down here called Mark, and James thingy has gone right out of the window. I haven't seen this Mark yet, but I've discovered that he's the brother of a girl called Madeleine, who's become Adele's instant best friend. He has another two sisters – one's called Marie and she's really stupid (her and her friend keep spying on me) and one is only little, about four.

Fancy Adele getting a new boyfriend and a new best friend! Some people don't know anything about loyalty, do they? She's been best friends with Marcia for ages and now she's just forgotten about her.

Anyway, see if it's OK with your mum for the 15th and I'll get my mum to phone yours to confirm times and things.

Love, Bev x x x

I licked the envelope and went downstairs to see if I could scrounge a stamp. On the bottom step, I heard Podger say, "Look at that! Well done, old boy!" and when I went into the kitchen, he and Mum were looking admiringly at Mrs Armitage's cat, who had three mice lined up just outside the back door.

"Look what the clever thing's caught!" Mum said to me.

"How disgusting," I said. "Poor defenceless little mice!"

"It's the law of the jungle," Mum said wisely. "*Nature red in tooth and claw*."

"He's turned out a real farm cat!" Podger said. "Who'd have thought a pampered pet like that could catch three mice in one morning. He'll be really handy in the barn, come winter."

"He won't be here in the winter!" I said, but they ignored me.

"Our Felix couldn't catch a bus! Useless, he was. Much too slow," said Mum.

"Our Possom *could*!" I contradicted. "I bet he'd be as good as any cat at mousing."

"Ah, but this one's a champion!" Podger said.

Mum tickled Fluffy Bo-Jo under his chin. "Yes, we like you, boy! We're keeping you!"

"We can't!" I protested. "What about ours? We can't just abandon him."

"We're not abandoning him," Mum said. "Mrs Armitage rang me last night to say she'd like to keep him. Apparently, this one used to hide under the bed for days on end and wasn't very friendly, but our Felix sits on her lap and walks down the road to the shops with her. She said he's become a real friend."

"That's nice," I said bitterly.

"She's renamed him Fifi la Belle!"

I put on my sourest expression. "Great,"

69

I said. So *that* put paid to my little trip to London.

I started to stomp upstairs again to rewrite the letter to Sal but then I changed my mind. It didn't really matter if the cats weren't going to be exchanged: that had just been an excuse. I'd arrive at Sal's without the cat – say I'd forgotten it. I just had to get there, that was all . . .

CHAPTER 7

Mum put down her paintbrush and looked quizzically at the design she'd done on one of the kitchen cupboard doors.

"What d'you think of that?" she asked me. "I used a stencil for the background and now I'm just touching up. I think it really brightens the room."

I looked at it. "I think you've been reading too many of those country house magazines," I said. "They've gone to your head." I began to slip away before she tried to involve me.

"I'm going to do a design on each of the top cupboards," she went on. "And then I'm going to do something round the mantelpiece. Beverley! Before you go . . ."

"What?"

"I've got someone coming to tea this afternoon."

"Oh yes?" I said, edging towards the door.

"Someone coming to tea with *you*, I mean."

"What?!" I said.

"A really nice little girl – I'm sure you'll like her," Mum said quickly. "I was speaking to a woman in the village, you see – a very interesting woman – and she said her daughter's been at the local school and is going to start at the comprehensive when you do. She's quite lonely too, so we thought it would be pleasant if you met each other. Her name's Justine and she's twelve!" she finished brightly.

I stared at her in dismay. Fancy having your mum going around trying to trawl up friends for you! How desperate could you get? "Mum!" I groaned. "What did you say to her? You didn't tell her that I didn't have any friends, did you?"

"Of course I didn't! She just suggested that Justine come over and tell you about school and getting the bus and everything, and then you can go to her house sometime and – well anyway, it *would* be nice if you made friends with each other, wouldn't it?"

I slouched towards the door. "I'm running away," I said.

"Well, run back by four," Mum said. "That's when she's coming."

I took the goats for a run round the field, and then I groomed them a bit. Grooming meant trying to stop them from eating the brush. Then it was nearly four o'clock so I went back in. I couldn't think what this Justine was going to be like – it was a bit like having a blind date. Worse. Imagine a blind date fixed up by your *mum*.

This girl would either be all horsy, I decided – she'd smell of horse-doings, have a head-scarf and a waxed jacket and keep clicking her fingers and saying Giddy-up – or she'd be frumpy with a scratchy hand-knitted yellow jumper over a baggy Crimplene skirt. I pulled a face at the goats; whatever she was like she wasn't going to be a bit like Sally and I was going to hate her.

She came while I was upstairs playing tapes, and I heard Mum go to the door and say, "Oh, you must be Justine. How nice of you to come!" in a smarmy voice which made me cringe. She sounded positively desperate. I don't know why she just didn't go out on the street and offer people ten pounds to be my friend and be done with it.

I didn't hear what Justine said in reply, but Mum called up the stairs in a highly false voice that Justine was here, darling, and to come down now.

I went. She wasn't frumpy or horsy or posh. She was about my height, I suppose, and she had short straight hair cut in a perfect bob that made her look really grown up. She was wearing a black lycra mini skirt and a tight

73

black jumper and she had a bust! She also had blue eyeshadow and pearly pink lipstick.

"Beverley, this is Justine," Mum said a bit faintly, and her eyes were all sort of glazed over with surprise.

"Hi," Justine said.

"Hi," I gulped.

"Do you want to show me your goats?"

"OK," I said, and we went outside.

"I only said that to get out of the house," she said as we walked towards their field. "We wouldn't be able to talk in there, would we?"

"No," I said. I was wearing jeans and a T-shirt and I felt all childish and stumpy next to her.

"Where's your brother?" she asked. "Is he around?"

I looked at her in surprise. "I haven't got a brother," I said.

Her face fell. "Someone told me that you had a brother. Sixteen, they said he was."

"I've got a sister – *she's* sixteen."

She looked really put out. "Marie and Gina – they live in the village – told me you had this gorgeous brother who played in a group. I must say I couldn't wait to get here."

I didn't say anything. Marie and Gina again! So that was why she was all dressed up like a dog's breakfast.

We sat on the gate and looked at the goats.

She tossed back her hair. "I mean, I have *got* a boyfriend but it's always nice to meet other boys, isn't it?"

"Dunno," I said.

"Have you got a boyfriend?"

I shook my head.

"Well, I don't suppose you've got one down here yet, but how about in London? I bet London boys are really exciting, aren't they?"

"Not really," I said.

She studied her fingernails: they were white, pink, orange, red and black. "I've been going out with Guy Peters for three months," she said. "Before that I was seeing his brother."

"Oh," I said.

"But quite honestly I'm getting a bit fed up with Guy." She gave a careless laugh. "Laurie Knight wants to go out with me but I'm not interested. He bought me a huge Valentine card but I said to him, 'Laurie, I don't care if you send me ten cards, I just don't fancy you.'"

This was so profoundly uninteresting that I couldn't think of anything to say, so just said, "Oh," again.

She sighed. "So I was quite excited when I heard you had a brother. I bet that stupid Marie just made it up."

"Sounds like it," I said.

"They're so jealous of me. They *never* have any success with boys, you see."

"Oh."

"They're such *babies*, those girls. They just go round giggling all the time and making up things – they think they're so clever. And they haven't got any idea about clothes." She shot a quick glance at what I was wearing and didn't look too impressed. "I thought you'd be really trendy – coming from London."

"I am!" I said. How did *she* know what was trendy in London?

"I suppose you dress up for parties. What clothes have you got? I've got some really tight leggings that Mum got me from her catalogue. And a top with sequins on it and a plunge-neck T-shirt that's cut right down at the back."

I didn't say anything. How *tarty*.

"My mum says I've got a lovely little figure and I ought to show it off!"

Yuk! I jumped down from the gate before I was sick. "My mum said tea wouldn't be long," I said.

At tea I heard about how many boys she was inviting to her birthday disco and the games she was going to play (they all seemed to involve kissing). After that she told me about her make-up and offered to find me the right shade eyeshadow, and then she told me that her lucky colour was yellow and that once a boy had bought her a dozen yellow tulips but

76

she hated tulips so she wouldn't go out with him.

At seven o'clock, when we'd watched a couple of Soaps and she'd told me ten times that everyone thought she looked like the glamorous star of one of them, I decided I couldn't stand it another minute. I went upstairs to find Mum – she was on the landing, sanding down an old box.

"She's awful!" I wailed. "I don't know how you could have invited her! Can't you get rid of her?"

"I didn't know she'd be like that!" she whispered. "What d'you want me to do?"

"Anything! Just think of an excuse so she has to go!"

Mum came down a few minutes later. "Perhaps you'd walk Justine back to the village, Bev. I want you in bed in good time tonight because we're ... er ... going to the market tomorrow and we've got a very early start."

I jumped up. Justine stood sedately, smoothed down her lycra mini and said she liked to get to bed early, too, because otherwise she got awful dark circles under her eyes.

All the way up the lane she told me about a holiday romance she'd had. We reached the beginning of the village and – oh horror – I realized that there was a group of four or five girls – Gina, Marie and a couple of others – hanging about in the paved area by the bus stop. On seeing us, they started calling and whistling and I went all red with embarrassment. OK, I knew I didn't have any friends down here, but to have out-and-out enemies would be even worse...

"Take absolutely no notice," Justine said. "This always happens. They're just *so* jealous of me."

I felt myself going redder and redder. I didn't like them, but I didn't like *her*, either. And now they thought I was her friend!

They called after us all the way up the road while Justine went on about boys she'd known, boys she'd seen, boys she'd dreamed about, until I felt like screaming.

"I'd better go," I muttered when we'd reached the green.

"You'll come to tea with me next week, then, will you? I'll tell you about the time I went to a summer camp. Forty boys and me!"

"Mmm," I said.

I left her near her house and, just as I was panicking about having to go past the girls again, Mum drove up in Podger's Land-Rover to collect me.

It was too noisy to talk while we were driving, but as soon as we were parked in the yard I turned on Mum accusingly.

"How *could* you!" I said. "She was *awful*!"

"Sorry, love," Mum said, shaking her head. "I didn't realize."

"All she talked about was boys! And she only came here because she'd heard I had a brother!"

"Twelve going on twenty," Mum said. "And she sounded such a nice girl."

"It's obvious why she's lonely!" I burst out. "None of the girls like her because all she can talk about is what she looks like and how many boys are after her!"

"Sorry," Mum said again. "I was only trying to help. I won't do it again."

"And now everyone in the village has seen me with her and thinks we're friends and they'll hate me all the more!"

"Of course they won't!" Mum tried to reach out to pat my head but I jerked away. "Just give it time, darling. Another month and you'll be starting school and everything will fall into place."

"It won't! Why do you keep pretending it will?" I jumped out and stomped into the house.

Mum ran after me. "Don't go into the living room just yet, Bev!"

"Why not?" I said indignantly. If I didn't have a friend, at least I could have the telly.

"Because Mark's just come round and Adele and he are in there on their own," she whispered.

"What are they *doing*?"

"Just chatting. Give them another ten minutes or so and then perhaps you'd like to take them in some coffee."

"Perhaps I wouldn't!" I said, going up to my room with the double hump. Everything was awful. Oh, when was Sally going to write?

CHAPTER 8

"The surprise is here!" Mum called up the stairs, earlyish one morning. "Come out and see!"

When I went down Adele was already outside, and Podger was standing in the yard chatting to a delivery man, who'd just brought in a big box.

"Guess what!" Mum said. "Come into the small shed. It's all ready for them."

Mystified, I followed her into one of the sheds. Podger had been in there a lot the day before, setting something up – some equipment he'd hired, Mum said – and now there was a square table thing standing there. It had a guard running all round it, thick see-through plastic over and a big domed light on top.

Of course, when Podger came in with the box and it was *cheeping*, we knew what the surprise was. He raised the plastic lid of the table thing, put the light on, then lifted the chick-box in and shook it gently so that the chicks streamed out, cheeping and scurrying into their new, warm incubator.

"Aah..." I said, and so did Mum and Adele, and we were all smiling all over our faces in a silly way. They *were* lovely, though. I hadn't been much impressed with cows or goats (and especially not with geese), but these were so sweet: all fluffy and bright yellow and just like the ones you get peeping out of Easter eggs.

"I'll look after them!" Adele said quickly.

"No, I will!"

"You can take it in turns," Podger said.

"When they're big enough," said Mum, "they can run round the yard and we'll have lovely new-laid eggs for breakfast!" She threw a handful of feed to them. "We're just going to keep a dozen or so, just to be homely. I don't intend to go into commercial egg production."

We stood and watched them scrabbling over each other to get to the food. They were really cute. They fell around, picked themselves up and fluffed their little wings, cheeping all the time.

"It'll be just like the old days, when I was a youngster," Podger said suddenly. "We always had a few chickens then."

"Why are you getting all these things now

— I mean the chicks and the goats?" Adele asked.

"Because now I've got a proper family we can have a proper farm," Podger said, going red, as he went back into the house.

Mum looked after him fondly. "There you are," she said. "He's so pleased to have us here."

Adele and I stayed watching the chicks for ages, and then she thought she'd better clear up her bedroom because Madeleine was coming. She went in and I followed.

"How did you get on with Mark the other night, then?" I asked her daringly as we went upstairs.

"What's it got to do with you?" she snapped.

"That's nice! I make a kind, sisterly enquiry and you bite my head off."

She looked me up and down. "Have you seen my red leather belt?"

"No," I said, surreptitiously pushing down my sweatshirt with my elbow.

"I bet you have. I'm going in your bedroom to look for it, and if I find it you'll be in big trouble."

The minute she disappeared into my bedroom I whipped the belt off, coiled it neatly and put it on one of her shelves. Then I followed her into my room.

"So is it all finished with James thingy, then?"

She was peering into corners, under clothes, even behind the curtains. "As I said before, what's it got to do with you?"

"I just want to know if you're definitely not coming back to London for a weekend."

"I'm sure you've got my belt," she said. I haven't seen it since we moved."

"Are you or aren't you?" I persisted.

She strode back into her bedroom with me trailing behind her. "No, I'm not," she said shortly.

"Oh. So you're not heartbroken about James any more and you're not going to die without him and all that."

"Didn't say I was."

"You said you. . ."

She began to close her bedroom door on me. "If you don't mind, I want to clear up. Madeleine will be here in a minute."

"You said you couldn't bear to leave him!" I said quickly, through the fast-closing door.

"You couldn't possibly understand. You're just a *child*. Now go away."

I pointed through the crack in the door towards the shelf.

"There's your belt!" I said triumphantly. "I told you I hadn't got it."

The door slammed on me. "Some heart-break!" I muttered, loud enough for her to hear.

I went downstairs for breakfast. Podger and

Mum were outside in the yard laughing about something. I got myself a handful of biscuits – home-made, of course – and then got the packet of muesli out so that Mum would think I'd had some.

When she came in I was just putting my (clean) bowl in the sink and filling it up with water.

"What are you up to today?" she asked cheerfully.

"Nothing," I said. "The same as every day."

"You could always go and lend a hand with the cows. They're going to start calving soon." Humming to herself, she picked up her paints and prepared for another stencilling session.

"And what are you going to do for the fete?" she asked.

I gazed out of the kitchen window, willing the postman to come back. If I concentrated really really hard then perhaps he'd appear round that corner with a letter from Sally that he'd forgotten to deliver.

"What fete?" I asked.

"Much Standwick village fete, of course. Didn't you listen to anything we said last night?"

"Not really," I said.

"Well, everyone does something," Mum said firmly. "It's the big occasion of the year. We get together with the two neighbouring villages and people come from miles around."

"From London?" I asked.

"Maybe not from London," she said. "But certainly from Taunton and Bridgwater."

"Big deal," I muttered.

"There are all sorts of stalls, and a tug of war and a couple of fairground rides and a fortune teller – and one of the farmers gives a pig for the pig-bowling competition."

"Well, how cruel!" I said. "Fancy bowling a poor little pig along the ground!"

"You don't bowl the pig, silly. You bowl *for* him – to win him!"

I screwed up my face. "Who'd want to win a pig! Suppose I won him – you wouldn't let me keep him in my bedroom, would you?"

Mum sighed. "You sell the pig," she said. "Or have it killed and eat it."

"How *horrible*!"

"And anyway," she went on swiftly, "you'll be able to buy lots of local crafts and there'll be a white elephant stall and different things to eat and everyone dresses up and has a jolly good time. Oh – and in the evening there's a dance."

"What – a disco?" I asked, perking up a little.

"No, silly – a barn dance."

"How *embarrassing*!" I said.

"How can you say that when you've never been to one?"

"I've seen them on TV. You have to wear a check dress. . ."

"Roger *will* look nice!" Mum laughed.

"And dance round a man on a straw thing who calls things out. You wouldn't get me going to one in a hundred years. And you wouldn't get me helping at a feet, either," I said, deliberately mispronouncing it.

"You'll feel left out if you don't," Mum said. "Everyone else in the village will be doing something."

"What are you doing, then?" I asked, pushing biscuits into my pockets.

"I haven't decided whether to tie up my herbs into bunches and sell them, or to buy some pine boxes and stencil them, or just to help out on someone else's stall. Adele and Madeleine are going to run a second-hand clothes stall."

"Yuk! Fancy selling other people's dirty old clothes!"

Mum stretched to paint a leaf on the top cupboard and stood back to admire what she'd done. "It's all for a good cause, darling."

"What good cause? I can think of one – sending people who don't want to be here back to London."

Mum tutted. "Don't be silly! It's for the new community hall."

"Community hall. That sounds exciting," I said, wandering out. The postman wasn't going to come back. Who was I kidding?

CHAPTER 9

A few mornings later I went out to the shed and lifted the lid of the incubator. Carefully, I picked out two chicks – they were already getting bigger – and sat down on the floor with them. They ran over my legs and found something to peck at on the floor, cheeping all the time. They were really cute: the one thing I quite liked about living on a farm. If Sally was to come down and see them she'd love them . . .

One of the chicks ran behind some piled-up bales of hay and I left it for a while, but when it didn't appear again I decided that I ought to go after it in case it found a hole and got out. Podger had said they must never be left out because of rats.

I put the other one back and crawled along behind the hay. I saw the chick right at the end of the tunnel. I crawled a bit further and the top bale wobbled, overbalanced and fell on me, squashing me flat and coating me with a million bits of dust and chaff. Clutching the chick and coughing like mad, I crawled out backwards. When I sat up on my heels and tried to rub some of the bits out of my eyes, I heard someone giggling.

I looked round quickly and it was that Marie, actually *inside* our barn, standing laughing at me. I felt really stupid – and furious. What a cheek! She was actually spying on me in my own barn!

"If you could just see what you look like!" she said.

"You don't look so hot," I said coldly, because she was wearing a T-shirt with *Save the Whales* on it. "They went out years ago."

Instead of looking insulted, she just grinned.

"I suppose you've come to spy on me again," I said, glowering at her. "Haven't you got anything better to do?"

I put the chick back; it had pooed down my arm while I'd been holding it and I bet she'd noticed. "I'd just like you to know that I think you and your friend are utterly childish," I said in as a superior voice as I could manage. "*Quite pathetic.*"

And with that I marched out, leaving her standing there.

I ran upstairs to my room two at a time, shedding bits of hay all the way, and peered into the yard from behind the curtain, but there was no sign of her. Her and stupid Gina had probably gone to find someone else to spy on – or they'd gone to report back on me to their other friends.

A wave of misery swept over me. How could I start at school with them in a few weeks' time? How could I start at a school where *no one* was going to talk to me? I sighed heavily, grossly sorry for myself, and was just about to fling myself down on the bed and wallow in self-pity when Mum came in.

"Look at the state of you! Whatever have you been doing?" she said.

I didn't reply. It was all *her* fault. Why couldn't she have found an ordinary man? Someone who lived in London. Weren't there enough people to choose from *there*?

"Did you see Marie?" she asked. "Did she like the chicks? Why didn't you ask her in?"

"What d'you mean? Why should I have asked her in?" I said, feeling myself going red. "She only came here to spy on me."

"Whatever are you talking about – *spying*? Didn't you speak to her?" Mum said in exasperation. She moved around my room, picking up clothes.

"I did – sort of . . ." I said.

"What d'you mean, 'sort of'? She came along with Madeleine – she wanted to know if you'd like to help run a stall at the fete with her and her friend."

I stared at Mum. "Was her friend with her?"

"No – I just said, she came with her sister. She thought you might like to lend a hand with the hot dog stall they're running. Wasn't that nice of her?"

"I . . . I . . ." I stuttered.

Mum went out with a couple of Adele's T-shirts over her arm. "I hope you said yes, Beverley," she said sternly. "It was good of her to think of you and it's just the opportunity you need."

The door closed behind her and I sat down on the bed heavily. So Marie hadn't been spying on me. She'd come on her own to be friendly, to ask me to do something with her and Gina – and I'd bawled her out. I hadn't given her a chance to speak. I'd told her she was childish and pathetic. And now I bet she'd tell everyone that I didn't want to do a stall and I'd been nasty to her and no one would *ever* want to be friends with me . . .

I decided to go down and tell Mum what had happened. She tutted a bit, then she said she'd think of something; a bit later she called me down again.

91

"Madeleine and Marie's mum is one of the fete organizers, so I've written her a letter and you can deliver it. With a bit of luck you'll see Marie and you can clear the air."

"I can't. . ." I wailed.

"Of course you can!" Mum said briskly. "Now, I've written to Mrs March telling her that I'm going to make some old-fashioned lavender bags for the craft stall and that I'm quite prepared to help out on any stall in the afternoon. I've also asked her to reserve us four tickets for the barn dance in the evening."

"What?!"

"The whole village goes," she said firmly. "You'll enjoy it!"

"Whether you want to or not," I muttered as she handed me the letter.

I walked down to the village, gloom hanging over me like a cloud. I didn't really *want* to be friends with this Marie, this girl I hardly knew. Why was I going to try and make friends with someone I didn't like? Anyway, she already had lots of friends: she wouldn't have room for me.

I passed Justine. She was coming out of the village shop with two boys in tow.

"Oh, hi!" she called to me.

"Hi," I mumbled.

"That's Beverley," I heard her saying to the boys, and then she said something which I couldn't hear and they both laughed.

I scurried on quickly and crossed the green to Marie's house. Love-of-Adele's-life Mark came out as I got there and sauntered down the road, whistling. By the way he kept smoothing back his hair and looking at his reflection in car windows I could see that he really fancied himself. He looked a lot like James thingy, actually – leather jacket and all. I could hardly tell the difference.

My knees felt a bit shaky as I tapped quietly on the March's door. With a bit of luck no one would hear me and I could just push the letter through and run home again.

Someone did hear me, though. Mrs March opened the door and smiled at me enquiringly.

"Letter from my mum about the fete," I said, shoving it into her hands.

"Thank you, dear," she said. "I know who you are, of course – Adele's sister. You look just the same!"

I stared at her, deeply offended.

"You haven't got the freckles but your hair's got a lot of that lovely red in it! It's not quite your sister's colour but – well, we can't all be blessed, can we?"

I smiled glassily, wanting to say that I would rather be bald than *blessed*, as she put it.

"Do come in," she said, just as I was backing off. "I think my Marie wanted to speak to you about her stall at the fete."

Reluctantly, I followed her into the kitchen. At least Marie hadn't told her that she'd already been down, then – and that I'd been rude to her.

"Cup of tea?" she asked, and I explained that I only liked orange.

"Marie's always talking about you, you know. She opened the fridge and took out a carton of orange juice.

"She's absolutely green with envy about your clothes. I had to take her into Taunton last week and spend a fortune on new trainers – all thanks to you!"

I grinned to myself as I took a swig of orange. This was good news – at least people had noticed the things I was wearing were different from the things *they* were wearing...

"Mum!" Marie said, appearing round the door, hair all bushy and looking a bit red in the face. "I wish you wouldn't tell people things like that."

"Oh, no harm!" her mum said, laughing.

"No harm to *you*," she said. "Hi," she said to me.

"Hi," I said back.

"Want to come upstairs and see my tape collection?"

I nodded and followed her up the stairs, glad that her friend Gina didn't appear to be there. One of them at a time was enough.

"*Mark's* tape collection!" her mum shouted after her.

"He's given them all to me! He's buying a CD player!" Marie shouted back.

Her bedroom was a mess. Nearly as bad as mine had been in the old house. There were two wardrobes, two lots of bookshelves, four chests of drawers, two beds – and a thousand bits of clothing scattered over everything.

"It's really crowded in here because I have to share with Maddy," she said. She pointed to a white stripe painted across the floor. "My bit's over this side."

"You have to go in her bit to get in and out, though."

"And she has to get in my bit to look out of the window," she said. "So we're even."

I took a deep breath and sat down on her bed. "I'm sorry I was horrible this morning," I said quickly. "I just . . . it just felt as though every time I did something stupid you were there watching me."

She grinned. "It's OK," she said. "And Gina and I aren't really following you about – it's just that . . . well, in a place like this you can't help falling over each other."

"If you want me to . . . I wouldn't mind helping you on your stall at the fete," I said. There, I'd said it. I pushed down all the things I'd said to Mum about fetes. "It sounds quite a laugh," I lied.

"It'll probably mean doing something awful like slicing onions for the hot dogs," she said. "All the good jobs are gone."

"That's OK. I don't mind," I heard myself saying.

"That's settled then," she said. She dug into a heap of tapes. "Now, what sort of music d'you like?"

I stayed about an hour and when I got back Mum was sweeping the yard. She turned round and beamed at me.

"All right?" she asked.

I nodded. Marie *had* been all right, actually. Quite reasonable. And we'd found quite a lot to talk about. I'd told her things about London and she'd told me gossipy things about the village and about the school we'd be going to – it would be her and Gina's first term, as well. I'd made quite sure that she knew that Justine's coming over hadn't been my choice; that she'd been forced upon me by my mum.

"I told you you'd like her!" Mum said. "She seems a very nice girl."

"I didn't say I *liked* her," I said cautiously, "I just said she was all right."

CHAPTER 10

I stared at the chicks in horror. I couldn't believe it; they'd been *transformed*. Instead of fluffy little darling yellow things, they were now scrawny, half feather, half pink-skinned freaks. And it had only been two days since I'd seen them! Oh, I'd noticed that they were getting bigger, but they'd still been cute. Now suddenly they weren't. Now they looked like ET.

I went in to complain to Mum.

"Things do grow," she said wisely. "Animals, children, chicks..."

"But they were so sweet," I said, "and now they're all scrawny and horrible."

"You were all sweet once. A dear little pink, sweet-smelling chubby baby..."

"Do leave off," I said.

"And look at you now," she finished.

"Anyway, the chicks will be nicer when they're fully grown. They can come out of the incubator soon and before you know it they'll be clucking round the yard, all fat and happy, laying us lots of lovely brown eggs."

"Why can't things stay as they are...?" I said mournfully.

"Because life would be boring!" She moved into what used to be a utility room but had now been turned into a study. "I'm going to put the milk yield on the computer. Why don't you come and help? You'd probably be better at it than I am."

"Can't be bothered," I said. "Anyway, I'm meeting Gina and Marie down in the village. Some of the fete stuff is arriving on the village green and we want to watch."

"Marie and Gina! There, isn't that nice!" Mum said, and I pretended not to hear her.

I went upstairs and changed into my *No Worries* T-shirt and when I went down again Mum was chatting on the phone. I'd heard it ring while I'd been upstairs but I'd taken no notice. It had never yet been for me.

Mum waved and mouthed something at me. "Lovely! You sound as if you're having a good summer!" she said down the phone. Then she grabbed me as I walked past. "It's Sally for you!"

I stared at her. *Sally!* I'd almost given up hope of ever hearing from her again...

"Well, d'you want to speak to her or not?" Mum said, waving the receiver at me.

I grabbed it. "Hello?!" I said, not honestly believing that it was really her.

"Hi!"

"It *is* you, then,"

"Of course it is. Who did you think it was?"

"I wasn't sure. It's so long since I heard from you. I've been waiting for a letter," I said pointedly.

"Well, I never was much good at writing letters, was I? How are you doing, anyway?"

"Oh, brilliant," I said in a non-brilliant voice. I turned my back on Mum and she retreated to the kitchen.

"Is it really awful down there?" Sally asked in a jolly voice.

"Just boring," I said. "It is when you don't know anyone and there isn't anything to do."

She tutted. "Pity you couldn't have stayed here for the summer!"

"It was, wasn't it?" I said, thinking that I hadn't been asked. I hadn't even been asked for a *weekend*.

"We've been out nearly every day!"

"We?" I asked sharply.

"Me and Donna and Roselle. I'm round at Roselle's now. Her mum's gone out for the day and – you know her dad's got a company phone? – we've been on it since nine o'clock!"

"Oh," I said. She wasn't even at home, then, phoning because she missed me, or to arrange for me to come and see her. I was just someone she'd rung because they had a freebie phone. One of a long line of people.

"I'm not sure what we're going to do about the cat now," I said, just to bring up the subject of coming on visits. . .

There was a giggle. "Get off!" she said to someone. "Oh yes," she said to me. "I heard that Mrs Armitage wants to keep your one!" "And because she does, that's my coming-to-London excuse gone."

"Yeah. It's a shame," Sal said vaguely. "Get off, Ros. I mean it!" There were a couple of high-pitched giggles. "Roselle's got this feather duster she keeps sticking down our necks," Sal explained.

"Really?" I said, laughing falsely. Roselle always *had* gone in for stupid pranks like that.

"We're going to the cinema later. Have you seen that new animals in space one?"

"Haven't even seen a cinema since we arrived," I said. "They don't have them down here."

"Well, it's really good. We haven't actually been out to see a film for ages, actually. Not since the new video place opened. I told you about that, didn't I?"

100

"Mmm," I said. She started going on about the videos they'd all watched together while I wondered whether to mention again about going up. What if I actually asked and she said no...?

After she'd finished telling me about the videos, I had to speak to Donna, then Roselle – who managed to tell me three times that it was her birthday on Tuesday and she was having an amazing party with a real disco and coloured lights. Then Sally came back and said she ought to be going.

"We've lots of other people to ring!" Roselle shouted in the background.

"So ... well, are you going to write to me?" I asked.

"Not now I've phoned – I don't have to, do I?" she said. "I won't have anything to tell you for ages."

"Well, er..." I plunged in. "D'you think I'll see you before we go back to school?"

"Yeah, sure!" she said.

"Well, *when*, then? D'you want to come down?"

"I'll try," she said. "There's a couple of parties, though. And we haven't bought all my uniform yet..." her voice trailed off.

"Hurry *up*!" Roselle commanded from the background. "My dad will go mad if he finds out!"

"We'll have to get something fixed," Sal

101

said vaguely. "Drop me a line!"

"Bye, Bev!" I heard Roselle call. "Got to go now!"

"See you," I said to Sal.

"See you!" she said cheerfully.

The phone clicked loudly in my ear and I slowly put down the receiver. Well, that was *that*. The chicks had changed and my best friend had changed. I don't suppose she even *was* my best friend any more...

"I'm going out!" I shouted to Mum, and she reappeared from the kitchen.

"How's everything in London, then?" she asked.

"Oh, *great*," I said sarcastically, and she looked at me but didn't say anything.

I walked down the lane towards the green, wondering what to do about Sally. She wasn't going to ask me up there, that was definite. And unless someone went up there and kidnapped her, *she* wasn't going to come down here. Maybe I'd never see her again...

I didn't have much time to brood, because Marie and Gina were waiting at the bus stop. Everyone seemed to meet there.

I'd seen Marie twice since I'd been down to her house, but both times Gina had been with her, and it hadn't been so easy to talk because I'd got the distinct impression that she wasn't all that keen on me. I didn't much mind – I wasn't all that keen on her, either. She was really possessive with Marie – at least, she was when I was around. If we three were walking along together she always fixed it so that I'd be the one left walking in the road or the one who had to walk in front or behind. She liked to keep talking about people I didn't know (everyone in the village, practically) and saying things like, "Oh, Marie, didn't we have a good time when we went into Taunton/went to that party/went horse riding!" And then she'd add, "Of course, that was before you were here, Beverley," in the sort of voice which said that it had been better then.

I knew I'd just have to grin and put up with it. I'd have them to talk to when school started, I suppose. That was something.

"Our stall's arrived!" Marie said excitedly when I got to the bus stop. "And all the marquees and two steam engines and a few bits of fairground stuff."

We walked over to look at everything. Preparations for the fete were going full pelt and I'd begun to wonder what the village did for the rest of the year. All you heard was people talking about it: discussing what they were doing, what they were wearing, whether the profits would be good and if the weather would "hold".

"Sorry, but you *will* have to slice onions," Marie said as we reached the green. "But not all the time. We'll each have a turn."

"Justine did it last year," Gina said as we looked at the machinery for the fairground rides and tried to work out what they were. "She arrived absolutely dripping in perfume. . . ."

"And this really smelly handcream," Marie put in.

"So after a few minutes everyone started complaining that their hot dogs smelt of Ashes of Roses or something. . . ."

"So we asked her to go and wash her hands. . . ."

"But she wouldn't. She said it was a strong barrier cream to stop her smelling of onions because she had a date afterwards!"

"So we chucked her out and did it all ourselves, didn't we, Gina?" Marie said. "We got on much better; all *she'd* done was slice one onion and then spend half an hour posing in case any boys walked by."

We wandered round a bit, then they walked back with me because they wanted to see Griff and Gruff. When we reached the goat field, we saw Mark and Adele coming out of the house – hand in hand.

"It's my horrible sister!" I said, pulling a face. She wasn't in favour; that morning I'd tried to sneak a look at the clothes she and Madeline had collected for their second-hand stall and she'd practically shut my nose in the door.

"With my horrible big-headed brother!" Marie said. "Let's trail them!"

Gina groaned. "What *for*?"

"Just for something to do." Marie pulled at her hand. "Come on!"

We trailed them all the way down the road back into the village, hiding behind the hedges. Marie did some imitation bird calls and I made some false "baaing" noises (although there weren't any lambs nearby) but they didn't seem to notice. They were talking all the time and Adele was smiling her silly smile and laughing her false high-pitched laugh. Talk about *yuk*. Our game stopped when they reached the village because they caught the bus of the week – we found out later that they'd gone to the cinema.

Once they'd disappeared into the distance, we sat down on the wall near the bus stop.

"I might as well go back and have some lunch, seeing as I'm nearly home," Marie said eventually.

"You can come to my house and have something if you like," Gina said. "My mum's out."

I put my head on one side, pretending to look at the bus timetable and feeling embarrassed. Was she going to ask me, too?

"I'd better not," Marie said. "I told Mum I'd be in."

"My mum's left me pizza – loads of it." Gina

105

wheedled. "And we want to talk about..." she lowered her voice, "you know what."

I immediately felt terrible; awkward and out-of-it. It was that horrible left-out feeling; just how it used to be when Sally and I had rowed and she'd gone off with Donna or Roselle.

"Oh, if you like, then," Marie said after a moment. She obviously knew what *you know what* was. "I'll have to call in at home first, though."

"I'd better be getting back, anyway," I said, all casual and carefree. "I've got to ... er ... feed the chickens. See you later!" I put my hands in the pockets of my jacket (Adele's cast-off) and prepared to saunter off. "See you tomorrow, maybe."

Gina nudged Marie hard. "Not tomorrow," she said. "We're busy, aren't we, Marie?"

Marie looked at her in surprise. "What – all day?"

She got nudged again; I pretended not to notice. "Yes," Gina said, "we've got things to buy..."

"See you sometime, then!" I said airily, walking away quickly before they noticed that my face was red.

I walked down the lane back to the farmhouse, kicking stones and sending them skidding all over the place. Well, what had I expected? I hadn't really thought that I'd move here and find an instant best friend all ready and waiting for me, had I? Of course Marie already had someone . . . and of course that someone didn't want *me* around. . .

CHAPTER 11

I sploshed through puddles towards the barn, swinging my bucket of scraps for the goats. "Nice potato peelings!" I called, to give them an appetite for what was to come. "Bits of stale bread . . . old cabbage leaves . . . mouldy bits of cheese . . . come and get it!"

I pushed open the door and there was a squeal and a flurry and Adele and Mark sprang away from each other. "Do you *mind*?" she said, turning and glowering at me, and Mark turned and glowered, too.

"I didn't know you were in here, did I?" I said, waving my scraps. "Podger just told me to come and give this lot to the goats."

"You might have knocked!"

"Whoever knocks on a *barn*?" I said. "And anyway, if you hadn't been so busy *snogging* you would have heard me."

Adele gave me a drop-dead, withering sort of look. Then, as the goats dived at the food, she and Mark made a great show of sighing and huffing and getting up and going out, even though it was still pouring with rain.

It had been pouring for three days now, throwing the whole village into a state of high panic about the fete, which was the next day.

I watched the goats attack the food — they would have eaten the bucket if I'd let them — and then, pausing only to throw the teenage chickens some grain, I went back indoors. There was no sign of Mark or Adele. In the kitchen, Mum had stopped fiddling with the approximately two million lavender bags she'd made for the fete and was looking out of the window with a worried expression.

"I don't know *what* they'll do," she said, "but if it carries on raining it'll be disastrous. Every single Saturday up till now has been fine — and now look at it!"

I shrugged. "Can't people just walk round with umbrellas up?"

"It's not that," she said, "country people don't mind the wet. It's the things on the stalls. Most are uncovered, so all the crafts and produce will get soaked. I won't be able to put my lavender bags out!"

"If it's cold and wet, will more people want hot dogs?" I asked.

"Probably." She suddenly stopped looking out of the window. "What arrangements have you made for your stall? Have you seen your friends lately?"

I shook my head.

"Well, don't you think you ought to go down and ask what time they want you and if you've got to turn up in an apron and will you need rubber gloves and so on?"

"I s'pose so," I said.

"You can't expect them to run around after you, Beverley." She started to pile the lavender bags into a box. "You've got to go more than halfway." Meaningful raised-eyebrow look. "After all, it's *you* who's the newcomer."

"I know *that*," I said. Fat chance of forgetting it.

"So why don't you pop down to Marie's house and just..."

"I might. Later," I said, disappearing upstairs. Why did she keep on? Why was she always breathing down my neck?

I hadn't seen Marie and Gina since the day we'd followed Adele and Mark to the bus stop. Marie had rung me, though, to say that a woman from the Women's Institute – they sort of owned the hot dog stall – was going to take the money for us, so we didn't have to bother about that. She also said that Madeleine and Adele had arranged for our families to sit next to each other at the barn dance.

110

We'd chatted for quite a while and she'd been perfectly all right, friendly and all that, but she hadn't said anything about the *you know what* business, so I still didn't know what it was. Something secret and special, obviously.

I think the worst bit was not knowing. It was like when Donna had asked Sally to go away with her and her mum in a caravan. I can't remember why Sal had been asked and not me or Roselle, but anyhow it had been awful: she and Donna had whispered and written notes and giggled and carried on for weeks before the trip, instantly going quiet whenever I appeared.

I read the best part of a book, then remembered that Adele was out so it might be a good time to sneak a look at the clothes she and Madeleine had collected. I didn't really think there'd be anything I wanted, but I reckoned I ought to have a nose through them before they went on sale, just in case...

The clothes were in great piles all over her room: trousers, tops, dresses; different piles for men and women. I made my way stealthily – even though Adele was out, I was still taking my life in my hands – towards what looked like men's jackets. Ever since I'd seen a bunch of students at a bus stop in London wearing them, I'd rather fancied having a long black overcoat. I rummaged a bit and pulled one

111

out, but it turned out to be navy. While I was still rummaging, bent over the pile, the front door crashed open and, before I could make myself scarce, Adele raced up the stairs and burst into the room.

I put on my most innocent expression. "I was only . . ." I began, but she didn't give me a chance to say anything.

"I've seen a calf being born!" she cried. "It came out in a little plastic sack thing!"

"I just came in here to . . ."

"The mother cow burst the sack and started licking it all over, and the calf was all wobbly, and then it got to its feet and stood up all on its own!"

"Oh," I said, feeling dead jealous. I'd never seen a calf born except on *Blue Peter*, and that didn't count.

"It was so lovely!" she said breathlessly. "It wasn't ugly, like kittens are. It was really sweet, with great big eyes. It looked all round and saw me! I was the first human being it saw!" She suddenly narrowed her eyes. "What are you doing in here?"

"I just . . . just came to give you some more second-hand clothes," I said quickly. I put on a generous, helpful expression. "I didn't really want to, but Mum said it was for a good cause so I thought . . ."

"Where are they, then?" she asked.

I waved vaguely. "In that pile there. Just

112

a couple of T-shirts. I haven't got a lot of clothes, as you know, but I thought – well, if it's for your stall and it would help you out. . ."

She moved towards me threateningly. "You must think I'm stupid. If you've given some T-shirts, you just show me where they are."

"Oh, over there!" I waved again. "How did that little calf look then, Dell? What colour was it? Did it know where to go for its milk?"

"Out!" she said. "You've just been in here raking through everything. Being nosy!"

"I haven't!" I said indignantly.

"I don't believe anything you've said!"

I shrugged my shoulders and tried to look misunderstood. "You never do," I said sadly, moving towards the door.

I went downstairs to see if I could find a raincoat and wellies to go down to the farm: I wanted to see a calf born, too. I got all togged up but when I looked in on Mum she said that there wasn't time; Podger was coming home for lunch and she wanted us all to sit down together.

Over lunch, Podger said there weren't any more calves due that day (Adele shot me a pleased, smug look) so when we'd eaten, I decided that I ought to go to Marie's house and get my last-minute fete instructions.

It had stopped raining and I walked as far as the farm with Podger. I thought that I might as well have a quick look in just to make sure no calves had decided to arrive early. There were two hugely fat cows standing quietly in a nursery pen, but Podger said they weren't ready to give birth yet – and that anyway, they'd probably do it in the middle of the night.

I went further in, looking for Adele's calf (as she'd kept calling it at lunch-time) and found a tiny little thing lying down all on its own in one of the stalls.

Podger had gone off somewhere else so I asked Alf, one of the farm workers, if it was the calf that had been born that morning.

He nodded. "Its mother's not very maternal," he said. "She's forgotten she's had it, I reckon – she's wandered off with the rest of the herd."

"Do they do that, then?" I asked in dismay.

"Oh, aye," Alf said.

I looked at the poor little thing lying there all pathetic and abandoned. "How could she just do that? How will it feed?!"

"Oh, he'll do all right," Alf said. "He'll drink from a bucket when we've got time to teach him. I'll get round to him after this afternoon's milking."

I stared at the calf. "But he looks so . . . miserable. Can't he have some milk now?"

"You try him then, ducks," Alf said. "There's

a bucket of milk there . . . stick your fingers in his mouth first and get him to suck, then move your fingers down to the bucket until he's drinking from that."

Alf wandered off, whistling, and I reached for the bucket. *This was it.* I was going to save a calf's life.

I went nearer and patted it gently. It was a dear little thing, a soft black colour; and not a bit scared.

"Here we are, then. Nice milk," I said. "Come and get it."

I dipped my fingers in the milk and the calf immediately started to suck them, struggling to get to its feet. I dipped again, it sucked and I smiled to myself. We were getting on quite well – I was a natural. I moved my hand into the bucket and its nose followed, then it suddenly jerked its head up, banging the bucket and sending milk all over the floor and me.

"What did you do that for?" I muttered, brushing milk off my jeans.

Alf put his head round the corner. "They always feed with their heads up," he said with a grin. "It's instinct. You'll need an awful lot of patience to get him to bucket-feed."

"I'll manage," I said, tipping milk out of my shoe.

The thing was, the calf didn't seem to have the strength to stand up for long, but he couldn't drink at all sitting down – so in the end I had to move him over to the wall and prop him there with my knee under his tummy. Doing this *and* holding the heavy bucket at the right sort of level was dead tricky and it felt as if my back were breaking, but I was saving a life so I didn't mind.

For ages it didn't seem as if the daft thing was ever going to get the hang of it. It banged the bucket with its head so many times that before long my jeans were soaked right through and I had milk up to my eyebrows. I went to Alf for another pail of milk and kept on trying: dip...suck...dip...suck. Craftily I moved my hand down into the bucket, until at last the calf was actually taking the milk on its own, slurping and sucking noisily.

Finally it sank to the ground, satisfied, and immediately went to sleep. I beamed at it. Wait until I told Adele that I'd saved her calf. Well, not her calf: it was *my* calf now. I'd done more for it than she had.

"Done it!" I reported proudly to Alf. "He's taking it beautifully from a bucket."

Alf said I'd done very well. "Them Aberdeen Angus calves don't bucket-feed easy, they don't," he said.

"I'll come down later to see how he is," I said.

I had to go home to change, of course – I was beginning to smell like the carpet when

I'd spilt a glass of milk on it and not told anyone – and then I told Mum about my adventure, making sure that she knew that Aberdeen Angus calves didn't bucket-feed at *all* easily. I was probably some sort of genius at saving calves' lives.

I was just about to set off for Marie's again when I saw her coming across the yard.

"I was just coming down to you," I said, going out to meet her. "I didn't know what time you wanted me tomorrow."

"Well, the fete doesn't actually start until two o'clock," she said, "but Gina and I will be there most of the day, so you can come when you like."

I nodded. "Shall I bring an apron?"

"You needn't. My mum's got some of those big blue-striped butcher's ones so you can have one of those." She looked towards the barn. "Are the goats in?"

I nodded again. "We haven't put them out because of the rain. D'you want to go and see them?"

She said she did, so we went in and sat on straw bales.

"I thought I'd better come round because we hadn't seen you for a few days," she said, tickling Gruff – or it might have been Griff – under the chin. "I thought you might have changed your mind about helping."

I shook my head. "I only didn't come down

because I thought you'd be busy. The . . . the last time I saw you Gina said . . . I mean, there was something she didn't want me to know about, wasn't there?" I said awkwardly. "Some sort of secret."

She grinned. "It wasn't anything much."

"*What* wasn't anything much?"

"Oh, it was just that it was her birthday last week and she had a sleep-over, and she thought if you knew about it you might think you ought to come. That's all."

"Oh," I said.

"She wasn't allowed to have more than six people, and they were all invited already so she couldn't have you."

Griff/Gruff started eating one of my trainers and I pushed him away. "So what were the things you were going off to buy?"

"Oh, nothing much. She just wanted me to go with her and get two videos and buy the food and everything. You could have come with us, I don't know why she was being so funny."

"It didn't matter," I said, feeling better immediately – so much so that I let Griff/Gruff chew one of my laces.

"Well, I suppose I *do* know why she's being offish," Marie said thoughtfully. "It's because she might have to. . ."

But just as she was about to tell me *what*, there was a giggle from outside and we heard

118

Adele say, "Oh, do you really think so?" and Mark say, "Honestly, I've never met anyone before who . . ." and then the door was opened and they both stood there with their arms round each other, scowling at us.

"Not you again!" Adele said. "I can't go anywhere without *you* popping up."

"I like that!" I said indignantly. "We were here first!"

"Mum's looking for you," Mark said to Marie. "She wants you to take messages over to the men who're putting the marquees up."

Marie groaned. "I've been doing that all morning."

"So? *Now* you've got to do it all afternoon," he said, flicking his hair back out of his eyes.

Marie gave me a nudge. "See you in the morning – whenever you like," she said.

She went off and Adele and Mark just stood there staring at me. "Haven't you got anything to do?" Adele asked pointedly.

"Yes, I have actually," I said. "I think I'd better go and see if *my* calf's OK." I moved towards the door and paused for effect. "It's the one you saw born this morning," I added.

She frowned. "What d'you mean – *your* calf?"

"Its mother wandered off so it wasn't feeding, and no one knew what to do with it. I taught it to drink from a bucket."

I smiled pleasantly. "Alf said Aberdeen Angus calves are *notoriously* difficult. I managed it wonderfully, though. Saved its life..."

CHAPTER 12

"Beverley!" Adele shrieked from downstairs. "I thought you were supposed to be helping me? Where's the next box of clothes?" When I didn't immediately appear with it, her voice rose to an indignant high pitch. "Hurry *up*! Are you helping me or not?"

"Not," I muttered to myself, standing in front of her bedroom mirror and holding up an ancient evening dress covered in sequins.

"If you don't . . ." came threateningly up the stairs, and I hastily dropped the dress, took a box of second-hand shoes to the top of the stairs and slid them down to her. I didn't want her to come up; if she did she might see the lovely big and baggy black overcoat I'd discovered and quietly removed from her fete stuff.

Podger, Adele and I were loading the Land-Rover. We were doing it in a chain: Podger was by the back door, Adele was at the bottom of the stairs, I was in her room. There was masses and masses of stuff – not only was her room full, but she'd also hoarded a secret and locked cupboardful. (*Locked*. How mistrustful can you get?)

I lumbered to the top of the stairs with the next box, waited for Adele to appear and slid it down. She picked it up and passed it to Podger, but before I had time to pick up the next batch I heard Mum in the yard calling to everyone to hurry up and come out quickly.

I ran down – hiding my new winter coat in my room first, of course. Mum was standing by the back fence with an ear-to-ear smile.

"Come and see!" she called. She pointed over the fence where a small wooden-sided run had been erected. At the top end of this was a chicken coop (I was getting to know these country terms) and standing in the middle of the run, still looking gawky and ugly, were the ten chickettes.

"Look at them!" Mum said proudly. "We've almost got real chickens about the place. Don't they look lovely?"

I looked. They didn't exactly look lovely – more bewildered than anything.

"Will they be out all the time now, then?" Adele asked.

Mum nodded. "And soon they'll be laying lovely brown eggs for our tea. I want you two girls to make sure they're in the coop at night – because of the foxes – and I want you to look in their nesting boxes every morning. We'll have a competition to see who can find the first egg."

"Bet I will," I said quickly.

"No, I will," Adele said. "The same as I saw the first calf born."

"But you weren't first to save a calf's life," I said.

"And nor were you. All you did was. . ."

"Girls!" said Mum. "Please don't argue today." She looked up at the sky. "It's actually stopped raining – the weather's going to be gorgeous – we're going to take lots of money for the community hall – and everyone's going to have a good time."

I gave a snort. "I'm not," I said. "All I'm going to be doing is slicing onions."

Mum beamed at me. "You'll enjoy every minute of it! The old team spirit will triumph. Anything where people have all got to pull together brings out the best in them."

"Oh yes?" I said. I couldn't really see how slicing onions was going to bring out the best in me, but still.

Adele went back into the house. "What time are you off?" Mum asked me.

"In a minute, I suppose. Marie and

123

Gina are going to be on the green all day."

Mum put her head on one side and gave the *Fond Mummy* look. "It's worked out all right, hasn't it? I *said* you'd make new friends – and Marie and Gina are nice girls, aren't they?"

I nodded grudgingly. "They're all right."

"And at least you've got them there when school starts..."

I didn't say anything, but I knew I wouldn't *really* have them when school started, because they'd have each other. They'd sit together on the school bus and at lunch and in class and I'd be the odd one out, the outsider, the number three of the threesome all the time. And I'd just have to put up with it.

On the green everything was happening. I met Marie and Gina and we walked round having a look at all the stalls and poking our noses into the marquees. No one said hello to us – what they said was, "Thank goodness it's stopped raining!" It was like a catch phrase; right through the village, they'd all been programmed to say it. In the end the three of us came out with it, parrot-like, before anyone could say it first. We must have repeated it about a million times before the fete even started.

We decided we'd each have time off from the hot dog stall to go round on our own once things were actually up and moving. And Gina wanted to make sure that she and Marie were together – without me, I mean.

"Marie and I want to go to the fortune-teller, don't we?" Gina said, pulling at Marie's arm. "We went together last year and she was really *amazing*."

Marie nodded. "But then she turned out to be Billy Parker's mum so she would have known about us anyway."

"Never mind," Gina said. "She was still good. And we want to go on some fairground rides together as well, don't we? I'm miles too scared to go on anything on my own."

"I expect I'll be able to manage by myself for a bit," I said. "There's bound to be a time during the afternoon when people don't feel like eating hot dogs."

As far as I could see, Marie wasn't all that bothered about going off, though, because she just nodded vaguely. "Let's look in at the plants and flowers," she said, stopping by the flap of a marquee. "I want to see if my dad's won a prize for his dahlias."

We went inside, where it was hot and stuffy with a strong wet-grass smell. We found Marie's dad's flowers but they hadn't been judged yet (Gina insisted that they were *much* nicer than the others and were bound to win). Then we looked at the biggest onions, tomatoes, potatoes and leeks in the world

– but they weren't nearly as interesting as the *Vegetable in an Unusual or Rude Shape* competition. We stayed there for some time.

At about one-thirty we went back to our stall and Marie and Gina started slicing up rolls, boiling up frankfurters and filling up plastic pots with mustard and tomato sauce; I started slicing up onions. To begin with my eyes itched and streamed like mad, but by about the tenth onion they'd given up bothering.

At a quarter to two, our taking-the-cash lady arrived.

"Thank goodness it's stopped raining!" we chorused, and couldn't stop giggling when she said, "Yes, that's just what I've been saying."

She settled herself with some change on a small table at the end of the stall and began jotting figures down on a piece of paper and saying, "Thank goodness it's stopped raining," to anyone who went past. As I carried on slicing, more and more people arrived on the green and several were pointed out to me and whispered about. Also a dog was found with his nose in the frankfurter tin.

Dimly, in the background, we heard the vicar say he thanked goodness it had stopped raining and that he declared this fete open, and then all the hordes of people started milling about and we were in business.

I suppose nearly an hour had gone by and, as I'd got a small reserve mountain of onions sliced up, Gina said I might as well go off and have a look round on my own. "Then Marie and I can go on our own later," she added. I took off my apron, found my purse and went. I don't know what I expected – that I'd be wandering about not recognizing anyone and still feeling like an outsider, I suppose. But as I meandered in and out of the stalls, I found that I actually did know quite a few people – and everyone seemed to know me.

There were all sorts of sideshows – all the local clubs had a raffle or a tombola – and there were the usual things like fishing for plastic ducks and hoop-la and a coconut shy. There was the pig-bowling thing too and a wooden slippery horse you had to stay on for thirty seconds. They had everything, even special postcards saying "Greetings from Much Standwick Fete 1992" with a photograph of what I took to be a scene from last year's fete: the vicar judging a fancy-dress competition and awarding the prize to a child dressed as a boiled egg. I bought one to send to someone – Sally, maybe.

In the very centre of the green there was a roped-off area where, later on, there would be a tug of war, fancy dress and *Dog Most Like its Owner* competition. There was also a pet show in a small tent. This consisted of two cats, a couple of bedraggled rabbits, a hamster, a stick insect and something which I thought was a tortoise but which turned out to be a pet rock.

I looked at everything, lost a lot of my pocket money on a tombola, made a wide detour around Adele and Madeleine, rummaged through some old books, had a can of drink and made my way back to the hot dogs.

"We've been really busy!" Gina said. "But we managed all right on our own, didn't we, Marie?"

"We've nearly run out of onions, though," Marie said.

I took my place and started slicing again, people came and went and were served and informed how good it was that it had stopped raining, and the afternoon went on.

I was having a rest from the onions and was on plonking-dog-into-roll duty when Justine came up with a boy who, when he'd managed to stop burrowing into Justine's neck, asked for two hot dogs.

"Hello, Beverley," Justine said. "No onions for me, thank you very much," she added coyly, with a meaningful look at the boy – and he immediately said that *he* didn't want them either.

I did the plonking, Gina (on ketchup duty) did the squirting and handed them over.

"Thank goodness it's stopped raining," we all said to Justine together, and then we couldn't stop giggling at the baffled expression on her face. I suppose she thought we were having a go at her – which led her to drop the bombshell...

"I hear you're not going to Bigg's Hill then, Gina," she said slyly. "Whatever will Marie do without you?"

I stared at Justine in surprise. Gina not going to *school*? What on earth did she mean?

"Who told you that?" Gina asked her sharply.

Justine took a bite out of her hot dog and dabbed at the corners of her mouth with a paper hanky. "Word gets around," she said. "Anyway, you couldn't exactly keep it a secret much longer, could you? Not with school starting next week."

Gina turned away. "It's none of your business!" she snapped, as Justine swanned off, smiling, the boy in one hand and the hot dog in the other.

I was all agog with curiosity, desperate to know what Justine had meant. If Gina wasn't going to the local school, if she really wasn't ... then *everything* would be different.

"What did she mean?" I asked Gina. "Aren't you going to the same school, then? Aren't you going to Bigg's Hill?"

She didn't say anything for a moment and when she turned round she looked quite angry – though I don't know what she was angry with *me* for. "If you must know – no!" she said – and then she muttered something about wanting to see her mum, who was running the big raffle.

"Isn't she *really* going?" I asked Marie as soon as Gina had gone off. "Why not?"

Marie shrugged. "Her mum and dad want her to go to this posh boarding-school place and, because it's nearly in Devon, she'll be staying there all week and just coming home for weekends."

"Oh," I said, and as the news sank in I tried very hard to feel sorry for her – but couldn't quite manage it.

"I was trying to tell you – that's why she's been a bit funny lately. She only found out on Monday she was definitely going."

I nodded slowly. "I see," I said. "It's . . . it's a bit rotten for her, isn't it?" Rotten for her – but pretty good news for me . . .

"So, if you like, we can sit together in class," Marie said.

I grinned. "OK."

"And on the bus and that."

There was an impatient cough at the front of our stall. "Not very good service here!" Mum said. "Two hot dogs, please. Oh, better make it three –

Roger's just won the pig and it looks hungry."

"Has he really?!" Marie and I exclaimed together.

Mum nodded, and then frowned. "But do pigs like eating pigs, do you think?"

"If you don't tell it, it won't know!" cash-lady called.

Mum laughed. "Anyway, he's collected it and put it in for the pet show," she said, "so we might even win that as well."

After a quick line or two of, "Thank goodness it's stopped raining," from both her and cash-lady, Mum went off, and then Gina came back and she and Marie went off together for a little while. This time, though, I didn't mind being left out.

When my next break was due I walked about for a bit, lost more money on the tombola and then, by mistake, went within shouting distance of a certain stall and heard a familiar bellow.

"Beverley! I want you! Come over here a minute, will you?"

I went, dragging my feet. "I can't stop," I said to Adele. "We're really really busy with hot dogs."

"I just wanted to ask you – you didn't see a gent's black cashmere overcoat when we were loading the Land-Rover, did you?"

131

"Gent's cashmere..." I said thoughtfully. "Don't think so..."

"Only it was a really expensive one – it had a Harrods label. We had a buyer for it, too – Madeleine had mentioned it to the man in the post office and he said he'd give ten pounds for it."

"Fancy," I said.

"And now it's disappeared."

"I don't *think* I've seen it," I said, crossing my fingers.

"I'd know it anywhere," said Adele.

"But if you like ... as it's so important ... I'll pop home and have a quick look around," I added.

She looked startled. "I thought you were busy."

"I wouldn't mind getting out of the next lot of onion slicing. And, well," I put on a goody-goody face, "I don't mind helping you."

"All right, then," Adele said, clearly confused. "If you're sure you've got time. Look all round my room, under my bed – oh, and in the bottom of the airing cupboard." As I went off I heard her saying in a puzzled voice to Madeleine, "Sometimes that girl surprises me."

I made a quick detour via the hot dogs to tell them that I'd be another ten minutes, and zoomed off home. As I let myself in at the back door I thought for the first time that perhaps it really *was* home. If Gina was going to a different school then everything would be so much better; Marie and I could be proper friends – *best* friends, even.

I retrieved the overcoat – I knew I'd never get away with keeping it – had a drink of orange and was just about to go back when I remembered the postcard.

I sat down quickly at the kitchen table to scribble it to Sally. Under the printed bit – the bit which said, "Greetings from Much Standwick Fete 1992" I put:

Dear Sal,
    The fete's OK – it's stopped raining. Lots going on, have saved a calf's life.

Then I thought for a bit, but didn't add "*Wish you were here*", just:

Having a good time,
    Love, Bev.

MAD ABOUT THE BOY
Mary Hooper

For years, since her mother died, it's just been Joanna and her dad – and that's the way she likes it. Then Dad marries Tatia... Worse still, there's the boy: Tatia's son. Joanna is mad – and what's more, she intends to let the whole world know it!

"Brittle but bright ... very affecting... Should satisfy even the most casual of readers."
The Independent

THE BOYFRIEND TRAP
Mary Hooper

Arriving at her older sister's flat, with a bag full of teen mags and a head full of True Love, Terri is dismayed to discover that Sarah doesn't appear to have a single boyfriend! Something must be done – and quickly!

"A brilliant read." *My Guy*

THE PECULIAR POWER OF TABITHA BROWN
Mary Hooper

"I looked down at myself. I saw black fur. I saw paws. And I knew immediately what had happened."

Tabitha Brown is surprised to learn she's been left a cat cushion in Great-aunt Mitzi's will. But soon, the true nature of her aunt's legacy becomes clear. Landing on her feet, Tabitha realizes she has inherited a peculiar and extraordinary power – and she quickly sets about making good use of it!

Intriguing and highly enjoyable, Mary Hooper's story is guaranteed to make you purr.